More Praise for
BURNING GIRL

"Lightning pace . . . seduces you into canceling the plans you made for the evening."
—*Bay Windows*

"Spare . . . tight . . . mysterious." —*Bay Area Reporter*

"The way Neihart presents [his] moral dilemma is singular: it's well beyond the standard middle-class outrage at the wicked rich. . . . *Burning Girl* is about loyalty and the conditions that stretch it to its limit. . . . The prose pops." —*Gambit* (New Orleans)

"What a chilling little tale this is. Had me double checking the lock on the door . . . edge-of-the-seat material, and definitely provocative."
—*National Post* (Canada)

"Exudes an uncomfortable warmth like a feverish forehead."
—*Times-Picayune* (New Orleans)

"A certain page turner . . . well-crafted suspense that nails its twentyish cast in a late-collegiate moment." —*Paper*

"Chilling and delightfully lurid." —*Kirkus Reviews*

"Lean, intense and provocatively cool." —*Publishers Weekly*

"A great step forward for an author with a terrific voice and a strong sense of character." —*Sun-Sentinel* (Ft. Lauderdale)

"The climax is worth your wait." —*Out*

"A portrait of twisted passions and lust gone bad." —*Elle* (UK)

"Trash chic." —*Austin Chronicle*

"Between Neihart's sharp prose and largely amoral hip kids, you'll read to . . . *Burning Girl*'s jolting wrap-up."
—*Weekly Planet*

burning girl

ALSO BY BEN NEIHART

Hey, Joe

ben neihart

burning girl

Perennial
An Imprint of HarperCollins*Publishers*

A hardcover edition of this book was published in 1999 by Rob Weisbach Books, an imprint of William Morrow and Company, Inc.

HarperCollins books may be purchased for educational, business, or sales promotional use. For information please write: Special Markets Department, HarperCollins Publishers Inc., 10 East 53rd Street, New York, NY 10022.

First Perennial edition published 2000.

Designed by Oksana Kushnir

The Library of Congress has catalogued the hardcover edition as follows:
Neihart, Ben
Burning girl / Ben Neihart.—1st ed.
p. cm.
ISBN 0-688-15691-6 (alk. paper)
I. Title
PS3564.E296B87 1999
813'.54—dc21 98-42117
CIP

ISBN 0-688-17689-5 (pbk.)

00 01 02 03 04 ❖/RRD 10 9 8 7 6 5 4 3 2 1

FOR JULIE ODELL

Special thanks to Colin Dickerman,
Sloan Harris, Rob Weisbach, Ken Foster,
Sharyn Rosenblum, and the MacDowell Colony.

part one

1

Drew Burke, who was twenty, thrived in manly Baltimore. He told friends back home in New Orleans that kids were tall here, and strong. Girls were as buff, knicked up, and cocky as guys. Especially at Johns Hopkins, where Drew was a junior and everyone played soccer and blade hockey and lacrosse.

Keeping up was hard. The sports hardware, the cars, and the long vacations were out of Drew's league. To get by in plush style, he leaned on rich friends. They took him home with them to Manhattan, to Atlanta, to Naples, Florida. They picked up restaurant tabs with no fuss. They lent him their new Saabs and their new Navigators and their new Grand Wagoneers.

The car-borrowing was a thrill, but hitching a ride with rich kids was hell on your nerves. They didn't bother to call up and be apologetic. They didn't bother to say, Hey

I'm gonna be late, Drew I'm sorry, Hey I promise it won't happen again.

They'd just pull up in new cars that glittered like eyes, pop the passenger door open, and barely watch you climb aboard.

Today was starting to look like a waiting day. It was a late May afternoon. It was the Friday before Memorial Day weekend. Drew stood in the heart of the financial district, at the corner of Charles and Redwood, right outside the mouth of an underground parking garage. Bankers and biotechnologists swarmed the streets, all aglow, with flushed, smiling, good-fortune faces, built-up triathlon legs. The sky was deep blue with stray black clouds melting in the strong sun.

Drew wasn't bored by the long wait, thoughtless as it was of a certain girl to keep him on hold this way. He liked to hang out in the money bustle of any city; it lifted him up. He could imagine his twin, a new Drew in a devilish blue Helmut Lang suit, on his way to meet his broker for lunch.

He gazed up the street, where a brooding hot dog vendor with gold-foiled hair played house music on a boom box. The song never failed to swell Drew's head. It had warm synthetic beats. It had a diva singing, "Sweet dreams of rhythm and dancing . . ." Drew tapped time with his left foot.

As if on cue, a half-dozen young Alex, Brown brokers bounded around the corner, loosening ties and taking off suit jackets. The men were tall, an array of blonds. One of the fine young women was stockingless in black Gucci sandals. She smiled at Drew. Suddenly, he pictured her at his age. She became a humming happy beanpole girl with suntanned legs and a cowlicky blond Gwyneth close crop. The men lost years with her, turned into wide-shoulder soccerheads in plaid baggy shorts and gold hoop earrings and knotted sweaty rawhide necklaces.

Shoulder to shoulder, the brokers passed without a backward glance. Drew sighed. Now would be the cool moment for his girl to show up. Bahar Richards, he said to himself, come to Daddy.

The *chica* was supposed to be retrieving her car from this very garage, right here at the building where her boyfriend, Arnie, worked. She and Arnie had taken a long lunch at Kawasaki, nearby. Drew had gone on an interview for a third summer job in the neighborhood. So this was the perfect spot to meet. But where was she?

She was his best friend. Like Drew, she'd be a Hopkins junior in the fall. But unlike Drew, with his loans and scholarships and two going on three part-time jobs, Bahar was a loaded legacy: both her parents had gone to the medical school here in the early seventies. Dad was now a professor of cardiology at Hershey Medical Center; Mom, she was a shrink who wrote about depression and anxiety for a cunning fashion magazine, promoted remedies on CNN and *Today*, recorded thirty-second pep talks for radio news channels.

There was a brother in the family, too: Jake. Drew thrummed his chest with his palms and summoned that melancholy hottie. The two of them had been keeping time for six weeks now. Jake came to hard life in Drew's mind. He had the big knuckles, the long thick neck. He had heavy shoulders, dark eyes, a gruff run-on manner. When Jake argued, his whole body shook with passion. The way he paid close attention, it ran down your spine. The way he smelled, the way he smiled, the way he kissed, and so on, were narcotic.

Drew was sweating now, giving off a hippie aura: peppermint, salt, cantaloupe, oils he'd mixed at the mall. His smell rose to his nose, and he thanked God for the breeze off the harbor, a few blocks south. It was a licking fresh coolness in counterpoint to the sun that beat down on him. Maybe he should have dressed for the heat, but instead he had dressed for the cooler coming night in one of Jake's long-sleeved washed-thin Neil Young T-shirts, a Hopkins Lacrosse ballcap, long unhemmed khaki pants, and fucked-up all-terrain Nikes. Tonight, he'd be warm.

They were going up to Bahar's house, up in farmy Pennsylvania, where it always seemed to be cold. The parents were in D.C. for an appearance Bahar's mom had to make on *Larry King Live*. New book. Something about preventing nervous breakdowns. An eight-week plan. It was a big deal because she was going to get the full hour; she wouldn't have to share the spotlight with Calista Flockhart or Al Roker. She planned to talk about her own breakdown and how she'd cured herself, among other things.

Drew closed his eyes. He dug into his pocket, pulled out a bottle of pills, shook one into his palm, and swallowed it.

It's a nice thing to have, he said to himself, a best friend whose mom is a shrink. He turned his face up to the sun and lured serenity. And as he waited, the vendor's radio burst forth with a rap collage by a smoothie who rhymed, "Gotta/Prada bag/with a lotta/stuff in it."

The happy words made Drew smile.

2

Drew peered down into the parking garage. As if he might find Bahar lurking there. The ocean-wave echoes of prowling cars sailed up the cement ramp.

He turned away to watch the holiday exodus on Charles Street. Every intersection choked on minivans and Broncos and that new BMW 318ti hatchback. Cargo holds were loaded with bikes, sea kayaks, lacrosse sticks, water skis. Radios boomed beach forecasts and Steve Miller singing, "Time keeps on slipping, slipping, slipping . . ." Drew could see himself in maybe one of the new Toyota RAVs, stripped down to a white tank top or maybe no shirt at all, as if he had a torso.

Not that he was soft. His arms and legs were decently hard because he was in serious training for summer, for summer love: two-mile runs, pull-ups, crunches, NPR, vegetables and brown rice and tofu, Cokes if he worked late, weed if he camped, and totally no cigarettes unless he drank a couple of beers. It was crazy to fuck with your health unless you had money.

He was actually in training for Jake. To make himself a hardy, decent, dependable, smart, foxy boyfriend. Because Jake was coming on like a Hummer, and because Drew had no fucking intention of going another month all by himself—not ever. Aloneness was a slow fault that killed you.

Drew had known Jake for a year and a half. But at first Jake was just Bahar's brother in a black Volvo, waving hello as he did a U-turn in front of the house. Over the months, though, Jake had begun to light up when Drew came around, and their eyes met like hard little stars. Bahar had aggressively nurtured the union.

They'd been together for six weeks now, but at first they had just been comrades. They'd been fuck-around kissers, biting sweaty huggers. It was only three weeks ago, on the occasion of a sellout Jewel show at Hersheypark Stadium, that they really burned up.

It was a weekend during finals. Formulas wrote themselves all across the inside of Drew's eyelids. Cell Bio. Phys Founds.

Jake called him, asked if he could pick him up, take him out.

They sat high in the bleachers, to Jewel's side, and watched her on an immense screen. She glowed white on-stage, and even whiter on the display.

The music and the calm blackberry sky put Drew in goofy high spirits, and he kept punching Jake's arm, and Jake hit him back—not as hard as he could have, but still enough to hurt. As Jewel yodeled up on stage, Jake leaned closer so his brawny arm was pressed tight against Drew's. "I want to fuck you," he said in a plaintive voice.

After the show, they walked through the parking lot. Drew put his arm around Jake's shoulder and ran lines from *The English Patient* in a clumsy accent. "Let me tell you about winds," he said.

Jake nodded and put his hand on Drew's ass. "Screw the winds, man."

"There is a wind called the Jake."

Jake put his thumb down the back of Drew's jeans and steered him through the parking lot. "When my sister proposed that I like think about you in a different way . . ."

"She what?" Drew interrupted.

"Well she just opened my eyes," Jake said.

"She got me thinking that way about you, too," Drew said. "We owe her."

When they found Jake's Volvo V70R, Jake said, "I'm gonna die if I don't fuck you."

"Can't let you die, man," Drew said, and he gave up tongue.

They crawled into the back seat and unzipped.

It was the parking lot of the Hersheypark stadium. Jake smelled like bananas. He pushed Drew down to the seat and said, "I want to go deep inside you."

"Here, man?"

"Yeah." Jake pulled his dick out of his boxers.

"Man, *here*?" Drew was wedged beneath Jake with his back pressed against an old Igloo cooler.

"Sshh," Jake whispered, holding Drew's shoulders tight to the seat, kissing his neck. "I'll give you anything."

"I'm not the prom date, fucking dude," Drew said, getting his hand lower on Jake's back. "I mean, you don't have to strategize."

"Yeah, okay."

"Here, yeah, fine. What should I do?"

"Lower, my friend."

They messed around until two stoned guys in orange Polo Sport joggers wandered up to the car, tapped on the windows, and asked if they could join in.

"Chums, *no*," Drew said, rolling up the window.

"I wanna fuck the both of you," one guy whined into the small gap at the top of the window.

"You got a friend with you," Drew said.

The guys looked at each other and made faces before leaving.

"The tall guy smelled good, didn't he?" Drew asked.

"Well shut up about him," Jake said, and he pulled Drew's boxers off his ankles. He started to kiss the inside of Drew's thighs with slow wet lips. He licked under Drew's dick, down into the cut of his ass. His scruffy chin made wet circles down there, and with every light pass he relaxed Drew more, relaxed his insides so only his dick was alive, shooting straight up. Drew felt like he was an experimental plant. He was a sun-forced bulb. He was brighter, and freakier, and bigger than he would have been in his everyday life. He liked the difference.

3

Tires crackled across the pavement beside him. It was Bahar, in her forest-green Acura Legend. A doggedy old classic rock number played crisply on her radio, and she sang along with David Lee Roth and twin guitars and cowbells. She wore a second-skin white tank top that showed off her neck and shoulders.

Drew threw his duffel bag into the back and dropped himself onto the passenger seat. "Late, Bahar? Feeling guilty? Oh don't, please, not on my account. But baby I forgive you. Like I always do."

"I felt *sick*. I had to lie *down*." She tugged at the zipper on the side of her skirt with one hand; in the other palm she held a gold bracelet, earrings, a necklace. "But you look fantastic, I have to say. Mmmm. God, your skin looks so perfect."

Drew nodded. "That was unnecessarily nice of you. Thank you."

"Pshaw. As a fellow-traveler like fleeing just as hastily as you from high-school skin, I beg to differ."

Drew smiled. It was nice of Bahar to pretend that she'd had a pockmarked phase like his, but it wasn't true. She only said it as part of her mission to keep all self-doubt away. The psychic drill was completely addictive.

"I think I'm going to sign up for boxing lessons this summer," Drew said.

"You will totally kick ass," she said. "I see you headlining, at the Garden, against Prince Naseem."

"I was thinking more along the lines of getting in shape."

"That's just as good."

He looked her up and down. "You changed your skirt since this morning."

"Yep. I changed my skirt since this morning. I might just try to change it again tonight." She snapped the bracelet on her wrist and then put on her necklace and earrings. The car rumbled. "Where am I living? Isn't this America? I might wear five skirts today. I don't give a shit." She licked her lips and glanced over at him. A light pulsed in her eyes. "I know you've only met Arnie like three or four times, but isn't he the best? At work, today, he drafted a brief for a big merger that's going to happen, and he read it with me reading it over his shoulder, and it was like I understood just how his head works. He's totally confident in every line. As I got deeper into the argument, I became aware of his right hand and how it was cupped on the desk beside his telephone. Thick fingers. And the combination of the physical Arnie and the mental Arnie made me melt down to ore. I couldn't stop sweating." She pulled a photo, a Polaroid snapshot, from the dashboard. She kissed it. And then she dropped it gingerly in Drew's lap. "Arnie helped me change from my first skirt."

Drew held the photo in front of his face for a moment. It was smiling, naked Arnie. He had soccer legs. He had no tan line. Drew stared at the frozen Arnie in the photo. It was like the other few hundred that Bahar kept in a lockbox in her Lancaster bedroom—a morgue of Polaroid pornos. The shots dated back to her high school friends. Guys. Chicks. Some solo. Some together. There was even a sneak-shot of Drew, stepping out of the hot shower, dick in a handful of towel. There were moments when he didn't actually trust her with his naked image, but he had to admit that he'd never seen himself so jubilant in a photo. All of Bahar's Polaroids were full of that surprised joyousness. You could almost call them character references, Drew thought. Bahar had put these folks at their ease.

"You don't have to memorize it," Bahar teased.

"His dick's bigger than mine, so it's sort of a humiliation."

Bahar sniffed. "No it isn't. They're exactly the same size. I mean, they're different dicks. They're both great."

"Are you fucking him because his dick's bigger than mine?"

"Drew," she said, "I love Arnie. You love Jake. Each dick has a home."

As Drew flipped over the Polaroid, Bahar said, "I'd rather, um, that you didn't read that."

He read it aloud: "Wonder of wonders/I'm starting to betray a good man. 5/23/97."

"It's not what you think it is," Bahar said, and she tried to inch the car into traffic. A black Infiniti lurched at her, so she hung back, letting the Legend's engine labor.

"I think it is," Drew said.

"You're such a like hard-ass with me."

Drew sputtered. "I'm just dubious about how quickly you fused with this guy. He's older. And you've been alone for a long time."

"I didn't say I don't deserve it! Sheesh! I like when you try to be my conscience. Some of the time."

"Don't sheesh me."

She punched his thigh. "*George* Will."

Drew punched her back. She took it stoically and jerked the car through an intersection.

"Hey," Drew said, "what's the scar on Arnie's belly?" It was a thick slash, pink until it vanished in his hair.

"Surgery. He had . . ."

"Cancer?"

She nodded, biting her lower lip. "He had testicular cancer, honey."

"Oh," Drew said, and regret settled on him. He stuck the Polaroid back into its place on the dashboard. He slumped down in his seat.

"He's cured, Drew. Don't be sad. Like, cured. His plumbing is fine."

"I wish I hadn't asked. It's none of my business. I'm such an emotional illiterate."

"Not all the time." Bahar gunned the engine and zoomed into a sudden breach in traffic.

"But I'm getting better. You have to admit that. Since I gave up on my father, I really feel stronger."

"You *are* stronger. Since I first met you? Shit, you were pupa then compared with the man you've become."

"Don't overdo it, Bahar. I mean, to refer to me as a man just yet is a little premature. I just wouldn't want you to lose street credibility over it."

"Don't talk yourself down in my company. I won't have it."

Drew watched her drive. The impassive look on her face gave a thrill. She was working gridlock traffic without even frowning for the competition.

He touched her leg. "Hey, I *like* the skirt you changed into."

"You do?"

"Yeah."

She smoothed her lap. "Why do you like it?"

"It matches your legs, for one thing. It looks like there's a kind of gold thing happening with the thread."

"It's Dalal, baby. I am so into his work. Mommy got this from Lacey Houck at *Vogue*. She gave it to me last week. So I guess it means Mommy likes me this week. I just about fainted. Maybe that's why you like this skirt. Maybe you intuited that Mommy bought it."

"I just like the way you look—plus, it's very Mary Hong."

Bahar huffed. "To hell with Mary Hong. Did you hear me?"

"Yup."

"She's *your* friend."

"For sure."

"Ack, did she leave town yet? Isn't she like spending all summer in Boulder training for the triathlon?"

"Not quite," Drew started. "She's doing a Sierra—"

"Ugh," Bahar broke in. "Hardbodied cool playa Asian gal—my ass. She doesn't want to be an athlete. I don't buy her whole fake persona. So Lilith. She's an atheist, you know. All she wants is a hot look. I swear that's the real reason she's such a jock." Bahar stopped and gritted her teeth.

"Lady, your talk is lousy with mistakes, okay? Mary Hong is a devout, proud, strong, Church-of-God, brilliant, pisser-funny diva. I would think you could like be forbearing. Man, be forbearing Bahar why don't you!"

She gave him a curdled look. "No. I don't respect her. You'll be wantin' me to start respecting people left and right."

"God I'm a chilling prick to encourage such a loathsome code. I better look deep inside myself, huh?"

"Look! I have proof! She totally told me that she was going to read everything by Zora Neale Hurston this summer and then in the fall semester she's going to start having salon nights. I can just see it: Mary Hong, cross-legged on the floor in a sports bra and sheer Timberland shorts and she'll have such great *energy*."

"Just because she's ambitious and maybe a little bit silly at times is no reason to hate her. I mean, look at me. I'm totally an immoral fuck, but you've taken me under your wing. I mean that. If you can love me, you can't hate Mary Hong."

"I don't *hate* her," Bahar snarled daintily, pumping the brake pedal.

"You harsh on her because she's kind of a tall girl. So it's kind of jealousy. *That* is embarrassing."

"She couldn't *be* any taller, could she? What is she—five-eleven, six? I didn't see her on the South Korean basketball team, did I?"

Drew rolled up the sleeves of his long T-shirt. "You know, it is really ugly shit coming out of your mouth. Do you know what I'm saying? I mean it, Bahar. I'm asking you to stop."

Bahar, gripping the wheel tight and looking straight ahead at the sluggish line of traffic, let the words pour out of her mouth: "You like Mary Hong so much because let's face it you love all the Asian things in life, especially macho smart Asian boys who play a mean court of basketball. How does the name Teddy Cho sound?"

"I'm asking you to stop." He reached his hand across, touched lightly under her chin, the length of her jaw, then down the silky line of her neck.

She shivered.

"Will you please stop?" he asked softly.

"I'm *joking*."

"Well just stop anyway." He pulled his hand away.

"What?" she protested, cutting her eyes over at him. "What?"

"The problem is that Teddy Cho is just, in general, like the upstanding bloke who has a conscience *and* ambition *and* that kind of running effortless happy camaraderie with the fuckers he shoots hoop with. The way I explain it to myself is like, I'm learning basketball by watching him. It's the way if I throw football with my brother, I get better because I see the way *he* throws it, and my body imitates his body. But if I throw football with someone who sucks, then I just throw for shit. Do you get my drift?"

"Well," Bahar minced, "I'll give you a quiet quiet moment to daydream about Teddy Cho and his nice legs and the back of his, um, *neck* and the way he figures neutronic equations. I owe you that."

"Thank you," Drew said. "I thank you."

Bahar sighed and ran her palm down her bare thigh to the knee, as if rubbing in sunblock. Her nails were cut blunt at the fingertips and polished clear. She wore heavy black Gucci sandals with chunk heels that landed *clack clack* on the gas and brake pedals. She had a girl's summertime leg: taut tea-colored skin flawless except for a torn-open prune of a scab on the knee—where she'd fallen, jogging.

After sitting through two changes of the traffic light in the grizzled ornate gloom of Mt. Vernon Square, Bahar said, "Did you bring your black suit?"

Drew thought for a minute. "You know what? I left it at Micah Martin's house. He wanted to wear it on a job interview. You don't mind, do you? I mean, you bought it."

"It's your suit, Drew."

"Well okay. But I didn't bring it."

"Good. Give that suit a rest. Wear something of Jake's. Wear the Calvin Klein; it's tight on him. Maybe Saturday night we could drive to Philly for dinner. Like, Carolina's?" She made it through one signal, inched up to the Walters Art Gallery, and then stopped for the next red light. "I'm sorry for earlier. I don't mean to be such a cunt."

"That's not how I think about you."

"You don't?"

"Look, Bahar, I love you despite your foul mouth. But the way you *choose* to talk can't just smoke away because you say, Oh, I'm not a real cunt. I mean, I'm not going to lie to you and say, God I love when you cunt out on me. How could I say that? But I wish you didn't have to slash my friends to bits."

There was a long silence. Traffic lay in front of them like a stalled train, bumpers and fenders linked, engines slow.

After a while, Drew asked, "Did you call the doctor?"

"Yep," she said crisply. "I called him."

"Well it's probably just stress—right?"

"I don't think so. My period doesn't really respond to stress at all." Now she looked over at him, eyes brimming, and ran a palm up his arm. Her skin was like satiny warm water. She thumbed a big vein in the crook of his elbow. "I think I might be . . . with child."

"Baby, are you pregnant? Really?" He tried not to wince.

"I have to *see* the doctor first, Drew. There really has to be confirmation. Then I'll freak out. For now, it's all theoretical."

"So would you think about *keeping* the baby?" he asked. "Not a like impossibility in your situation."

"My situation? What—rich, indolent, insured?"

"I'm saying you have the freedom to choose," Drew said, voice rising. He turned to look at her. Why? he wanted to ask her. Why are you so hard? Why are you the way you are? She was a hard metal girl. So was that why he loved her? Was that how he wanted to be? Did he want to shine like her? Did he want her cold blood to pulse through his veins? It tempted him. His brain shivered and he felt darkness pull across his body and he wanted it to stop right away. He made himself sit up. He turned to Bahar with a smile and said, "Well I could *so* get into you as a rich young mom traipsing across campus."

She shifted into first. "Oh, I could *so* get into that, too. I so could picture me in a black Versace dress, laminated in gold as hell gold, walking across campus, carrying my baby in a papoose, a Dutch nanny trailing me with diapers and burp towels. And at every stop, I'd gather a crowd and tell chic baby stories."

Drew touched her soft arm and said, "On spring break, you can take the baby to Java and you're suntanned and you've got a really close friend along to keep you company."

"Oh," she said airily, "so that would be like you?"

"That would be like me," he answered, lazily sneaking glances at her lap. Her tan skirt just covered her panties, little bit of fabric flashing peach between her legs. It was hard not to picture Arnie's fingers down there, and his dick, thicker than Drew's, and his tongue. It was hard not to think about Arnie's hard dark fuzzy chest mashed tight against Bahar on that bed Drew loved in her two-bedroom top-floor rowhouse apartment.

"Are you checking out my legs?" Bahar asked.

"Um, sort of," Drew answered.

She curled up her lip, warily. "Why?"

" 'Cause they're nice-looking legs and I'm sick of looking at a traffic jam out the car window." He took a deep breath.

Bahar gave him an alarmed half-smile and pressed on the horn, swerving around a stalled taxi. She pulled next to an empty meter. The taxi zipped past. The driver flipped her off. Cars stretched a glittering line ahead of them.

"We're going to wait out rush hour," she said. "How's that?"

"What're we going to do?"

"Eat," she said.

"I'm with you."

4

The Ruby Lounge in late afternoon was black smoky tables and sofas grouped for four. It was nearly empty. The music was smooth and loud, old Sade singing, "Diamond life, loverboy . . ."

Drew and Bahar sat at the bar, waiting for the manager, Gere, to come out from the kitchen with their food order. Bahar had her legs crossed tight at the knees so her thighs looked extra lithe. Her calves were supple, tensed knots.

Drew finished a cigarette that he shouldn't have smoked, and as he stubbed it out he took a closer look at Duncan, the Scottish bartender, a newcomer this month, who hunched at the other end of the bar, taking beer inventory from the coolers. He wore a white, snug T-shirt with the sleeves rolled up the caps of his shoulders and dark jeans cuffed high. He sang along with Sade in a possessive voice and smiled at Drew when he got to the words "max-i-mum joy."

"Duncan," Bahar said, in a voice like she couldn't help herself, "I might be pregnant. Do you think I'd make a good mommy?"

He nodded. He went back to counting bottles.

"Possibly *his* baby?" Drew whispered. "How many weeks are you? It'd be a very pretty baby."

"Duncan don't want *me*. He might have an eye for *you*."

"Yeah?"

"Yep." Bahar slid off the stool and held herself still, with her toes together. She put her hands on her thighs and arched her back and closed her eyes. "I'm knotted up."

"Ya want me to help?"

She murmured, "Yes. Would you walk on my back?"

"No, baby. You're pregnant, baby." He gulped his Dixie, slid off his stool. "Want me to *massage* your lower back?"

"Yeah, honey."

"Okay." He used his thumbs and knuckles to massage low on her back and rested the side of his face against her soft shoulder. A couple of minutes passed. They swayed together as he rubbed her in a series of circles. When she said she felt better, Drew asked her to walk across his back. He lay down on the hard floor. She kicked off her Guccis and he pulled up his T-shirt. She marched her soft, warm soles heavy on his skin. Sharp bliss radiated out his fingers and toes.

Gere came out of the kitchen shouting, "Food!" and set three plates on the bar. She was a caramel blonde with the pert face of a French actor. She was a Hopkins dropout. She was rich. As far as Drew knew, she was the only girl in Baltimore who was friendly with Bahar.

Bahar stepped over Drew's body on the floor, leaned up to the bar, and kissed Gere on the lips. "I'm so starved."

"Me, too," Drew said. "Help me up, Bahar."

She ignored him.

"Please."

Still she ignored him, so he started to scramble to his feet. He was up on one knee when Duncan leaned over the bar, drowsy eyes half shut, and stretched his long pale brawny arm down to Drew and asked him, "A hand up then?"

Drew blinked. He saw long fingers, a thick wrist, and a veiny forearm. He saw the hair on Duncan's chest curled inside his white T-shirt.

"Um, huh?" Drew said. "I'm sorry. What'd you say?"

Duncan curled his lips into a smile. "D'ya want to stay down? D'ya want to stay on the floor or do you want a hand up?"

"Yeah, yeah." Drew reached up. "I want your hand for sure."

"Hoped you'd say that."

"You mean that?"

"Haven't seen you for a while," Duncan said. He closed up his fingers around Drew's hand.

"Been around," Drew said.

Duncan pulled him off the floor, pulled him tight to the

bar. At the moment their faces stopped just a few inches apart, he said, "I'd like to talk to you back in the kitchen after you eat."

"Really," Drew said.

"I want to ask you something. So come back to the kitchen."

Bahar looked over her shoulder at Drew. She nodded happily.

"Yeah," Drew shrugged, his eyes licking Duncan's great, red, wet lips and his perfect left ear. "I can be there."

Drew had only wanted to order a bowl of gumbo, for $7, but as soon as Bahar took over the menu, it was feast time. Now, nine hot plates sat in front of them on the bar.

The oysters were best, fried in a peppered batter with wasabi tartar sauce on the side. There were green chile wontons, and rosemary mashed potatoes, and fried green tomatoes, and baby greens in lime dressing. Black-pepper drop biscuits. Mango slaw. Some tarts.

Drew ate and ate, forearms planted on the bar, hardly pausing to suck on his beer.

Bahar picked at the food, sipping iced tea. She kept her palm on her belly the whole time.

When Gere placed the bill in front of Bahar, by habit, Drew felt his usual relief and swelling gratitude. It was gift-giving, plain and simple, and he wanted her to know how grateful he was. He wanted to kiss her. He wanted just to hold her and melt her. But he only said, "Thanks, Ba," and held her elbow for a moment.

She shrugged and said, "No biggie, hon."

The usual exchange.

"Well, anyway, thanks," Drew repeated, and he looked past her at the yellow polish of lamplight on the corner tables. The golden halo burned the dark air and lulled him into reverie, a memory of the beach, Florida, Ft. Pierce, a little fishing village. He could see Bahar, suntanned dark, hair slicked back with ocean water. She lay beside him on white sheets. A salt breeze eased the curtain in and out above their bed. Breakers lathered the shore. She let Drew kiss her stomach and her knees. She murmured softly to him. And just like that, the memory flickered away.

Now he sat barside. Now he tapped in time to Tricky on a loud stereo. The music was a fine hash of static and Chic guitars and a woman aloofly singing. Bahar played games with her jewelry. "You'd be crazy not to follow up with Duncan," she said.

"I'm solid with Jake."

Bahar shrugged. "Jake's great," she said. "I'm just thinking, you know, about the long run." She reached across, lifted up his T-shirt, and patted his belly.

Gere came back with Bahar's charge slip. She gave Drew a cold new Dixie. "On *Duncan*," she said.

"Wunnerful," he pretended to slur.

"Do you want to thank him?"

"I will. When he comes back up here."

"Why don't you go talk to him? He's back in the kitchen."

Drew furrowed his brow at her. "Okay, Gere, in a minute."

"Honey, can you *please* go talk with Duncan for a sec?" Bahar asked. "I wanna talk to Gere about something private. Do you mind, Drew?"

"Well yeah, I mind being ordered to do it at the exact time it works out for you. There are like ways to get people to do a thing so they can at least have the illusion of free will."

"Couldn't you fucking please go to the kitchen, Drew? I mean it."

Gere raised an eyebrow, but wouldn't meet Drew's gaze.

Steve Miller, in ripe voice, sang out on the stereo: "Really love your peaches/wanna shake your tree . . ."

"What the *hell*, Bahar," Drew said. "Since when am I on a list of valets and attendants? I hate it the way you said that. This is a public place. You shouldn't talk to me that way."

Duncan poked his head out the kitchen door, just as Bahar put a hand on Drew's face. "Is there a problem here?" he asked Gere.

"No," Bahar said, sitting up high, grinning. She turned for a look at Drew. "Baby I'm sorry. I was just like stressing for nada. Too much caffeine, maybe?"

"Uh, maybe," Drew said, still watching her cautiously. "Why'd you jump me like that? That was fucking spooky. That was like some Twiggy Ramirez scary shit."

She patted her chest, like she couldn't catch breath. "Sorry? Is that gonna work?"

Duncan pulled back into the kitchen, but for just a moment he watched Drew through the oval window. Then he was gone.

"You know what," Drew said, "I think I'm going to leave Bahar and Gere alone for a little while—'kay?"

"Good idea," Gere said brightly.

"But let me ask you one question."

"Okay." She put down her glass of red wine, leaned toward him with a smile on her henna-colored lips. "What?"

"Is Duncan single?"

"Um, far as I know."

"That's a good guy," Bahar said.

Drew turned back to Gere and asked, "How old is he?"

"He's twenty-six."

"Is he gonna hang very long in Baltimore?"

"I guess so."

"What else about him?" He cut his eyes over at Bahar. "I mean what's some cool stuff he's into?"

"Tell him," Bahar said. "It's like too perfect."

"He's into country music, the Miami Dolphins, Sylvia Plath's late poetry, and black comedians," Gere said listlessly.

Drew staggered backward from the bar, clutching his chest as if his heart had exploded inside him.

Bahar muttered, "See how perfect he is!"

"Damn," Drew said.

"What?" Gere asked.

"*I* am totally obsessed with Emmylou Harris and Wynona and, of course, I can't leave out Steve Earle," Drew said, pointing at her as if he'd just scored a goal off her. "*I* totally explicate poems by Sylvia Plath in my spare time. *I* am so far gone on Chris Rock, I've gone to New York three times to be in his HBO audience: 'New pussy can't read! New pussy's illiterate!' "

Bahar's eyes registered a slight flicker as she looked right past Drew. She smiled hard, baring her teeth like the dentist had asked her to, slid off her stool, and murmured, "Hey, look who it is: Mary Hong." She sauntered past Drew.

Gere lifted her eyebrows at him.

He twisted around to see the girls embrace. Mary's eyes found his, and she winked over Bahar's shoulder. Bahar was the first to let go. She patted Mary's side, turned away, came back to the bar with a blank expression on her face.

"I just figured that you were out of town," Drew called, and as he approached Mary he took in her whole look: Polo Sport running bra and shimmery green track pants, hair pulled back in a high wet ponytail, no makeup on her honeyed face.

They hugged, and she held him warmly, pressing her palms into his back, an instinctual massage. "No," she told him, "last minute change of plans, dude. I got a job at Hopkins Hospital for the summer, a paid internship in peds oncology. I moved in with Dr. Malcolm. I guess we're engaged, actually."

"Well fucking congratulations," Drew said. He took a

step out of her personal space, grinning. "God it feels so good to see Mary Hong by accident like this. Fuck yes! You look like you might have actually gotten some sleep. Are you all of the sudden getting like a full eight hours?"

"Um, try four hours tops. You know how I am."

Drew couldn't stop smiling. "How'd you find me here?"

"Um I was driving and saw Bahar's Legend out on the street. I just thought, Well, where there's Bahar, there's Drew, and I wanna say what's up to him. So here I am!"

"Mmm, fan*tastic*," Bahar called out, and she leaned forward on the bar to whisper poison in Gere's ear.

"Haters get deceased," Mary sing-songed.

"Pretenders choke every time," Bahar countered.

"Who?"

"I can't *hear* you."

Drew held Mary's shoulders. "C'mon, she doesn't mean it."

Mary shook her head. "*Your* fucking cross, friend. *Yours*."

"I know, I know."

"Okay, I'm gonna use the bathroom. When I come back, I have a thing to tell you."

"Ooh, man, a thing?"

"Be right back."

Drew nodded absently. He watched Mary jog up to the bathroom, and then he just looked over at Bahar and Gere, who were making as if they didn't see him. After a long minute, he said, "Honey, when you have absolutely *no* friends, I don't want to hear you cry. Okay man?"

"You make Mary Hong feel all tender inside," Bahar answered.

"Should I just go back in the kitchen and get immoral with an odd smarty-pants Scotsman?"

Bahar and Gere nodded without looking at him and kept on with their conversation.

"Bahar?" Drew said.

She stopped talking, and waited.

"Send Mary to the kitchen when she comes out of the bathroom, okay? I want to hang out with her. Okay?"

"No problem," Bahar said. "My pleasure."

5

Duncan was in the back office, behind the kitchen, smoking, playing Quake on the computer. As he tapped the space bar and slid the mouse across its pad, the muscles in his forearm danced. Onscreen, bullets flickered in time with grinding ruinous music. Drew sat in a plump office chair and rolled up beside him. "Howdy to ya, dude," he said.

Duncan turned to him and smiled. A cigarette dangled from the corner of his mouth. "You want me to start over so you can play it too? We could play against each other."

"Nah, I can just watch you play."

Duncan thrummed the space bar, saying, "Hey, can you take the cigarette out of my mouth?"

Drew reached over, plucked the half-smoked butt from Duncan's lips, and put it in his own mouth. "It's all wet," he said, shoving his feet under Duncan's chair.

"I slobber when I play computer games and when I drive."

"Well, o-kay." He thought for a moment, watching the side of Duncan's face, and then he tried to refer to Sylvia Plath in sort of an off-handed way. "This game is something maybe beautiful but annihilating, huh?"

"*Yes*," Duncan said, "exactly. I'm a Plath lover myself."

Drew sputtered a laugh. "I actually knew that."

Duncan nodded, tensing in his seat as a blaze of machine-gun fire filled the screen. "I'm just about done; you can play next."

"I didn't just gross you out, did I? That wasn't too stupid, and like too ingratiating? Was it?"

"Fuck, I'm dead!" Duncan shouted. He let go of the mouse and stood up abruptly. "Oh, I asked you back here because I wanted to tell you that you have a very pretty mouth on your face." He looked away and started across the room in a couple of long strides.

"Where are you going, Duncan?" Drew called after him. "How'm I gonna compliment you back? I'd really like to compliment you."

"Not necessary," Duncan answered without looking back.

"Compliments are definitely required in your case."

"Thank you."

"Come back and talk to me."

"You know what? I'm a poor man, and I've got to go back to my job."

"So?" Drew implored. "I'm poor, too."

Now Duncan turned, stood in the doorway. "So it's the dazzled brown girl who pays your way?"

"Look, I'm *really* poor."

"Yeah," Duncan said before disappearing. "And me—I'm a New Guinean warrior."

"Well maybe you are!" Drew shouted at the empty doorway. "You could be!"

Mary Hong came around the corner. "Huh?"

"What's up with people?"

"Like Bahar?" Mary traipsed across the room. She had long pale arms and a soft flat belly. Her legs were more built up, with faded scrapes down the front of each shin.

"I can't comment," Drew said, spinning in his chair. "You know my vows."

Mary leaned down to kiss his cheek. "Your vows. Yes, I think I *do* remember them. No gossip, no cigarettes, no poultry."

"Fuckin' A."

"Well those aren't my vows, and that clit just pisses me off. She just made some illiterate, bitter, harsh joke about Zora Neale Hurston and it really hurt my feelings. She so doesn't even *know* Zora Neale Hurston. I swear to God, sometimes I wonder if she even knows how to read. I know it's totally unChristlike of me to speak so shitty about her, but *fuck* her. Who does she think she's intimidating? I mean, yes, she *is* intimidating, sort of, because I guess you don't expect someone to be so openly mean, mean, mean. I don't expect it, anyway. But then I think: God I could beat her up so easy. Drew, she just sucks."

Drew felt quietly remorseful. "Baby, I know what you're feeling. Sure doesn't seem like y'all are ever gonna be friends again."

She sat in his lap. He held her around the waist, his dampish palms on her chilly damp skin. "I *heard* something," she said. "I'm not supposed to um tell anyone. But I want to tell *you*."

He squinted at the back of her neck. "Mary Hong?"

"Yes," she sighed.

"Mary Hong," he said sternly.

"Do you want to hear it?"

"Is it gossip?"

She didn't answer.

"Then I don't want to fucking hear it. Ya know, you had a set of steely vows yourself, when I first met you. Like, I'm so not the one who's going to question your devotion to God, but doesn't like God not want you to gossip?"

"What does God care about gossip?" she said. "Why would He be so petty? God doesn't have time for that bullshit. Why would He be God if He had time to catalog gossip?"

"No gossip. Period. Please. It's the one thing I don't do. If you take that one virtue away from me, I'm basically pure evil. It doesn't mean I'm against God."

"Well what I heard is more about Jake, actually, than Bahar."

Drew's chest sunk. He let go of Mary's waist, pushed her off the chair. "No, no, no."

Mary sighed, stretching her arms over her head. The angles of her elbows were perfect ninety degrees. She lifted up on tiptoes. "I wouldn't bet on my source, anyway," she said. "He's kind of an ill piece. Nice ass, though."

Drew reached up to tickle her sides. "You better go. Before I break down. I'm being attacked from all angles. You with the goss, Bahar with the boys."

She gave him a questioning look.

"You know what she does. She's always trying to throw me with new guys. She thinks Jake is bad for me. She thinks he's too big a player. She thinks he'll dump me hard. Which, of course, she truly knew before she hooked me up with him. I mean, I understand she's in a tight position. If Jake's making noise that he's restless, it puts her in the spot where she has to be loyal to him or to me. As far as I can tell, she's doing everything she can to make sure I'm not blind to Jake's potential shitheadedness."

"They're a lovely family."

"They've been amazing to me."

She shook her head. "I don't know why you love them. I'm sure I know what it's *not*. I'm sure I know that it's not just for money and pretty clothes. You've got to see more than that."

"I do."

"But what? Where is it? Where's the pulse?"

Drew sat up straight in the chair. "Man, how'm I supposed to explain devotion? I don't *understand* loyalty myself. It's just how I feel about her. And him. I wish I could say it better." He threw himself out of the chair onto the floor. "You know how much I love you and respect you and feel like I'm a part of your life. I'm not sure why you feel so like compelled to tear Bahar down. Mary, I'll tell you straight up: Since when is casual bitchery such a crime? I can name a hundred folks who've made careers out of it."

Mary spun in a circle. When she stopped, she peered down at him, smiling. "You don't have to. I'm gonna believe you." She held her chin with both hands and gave her neck a sudden chiropractic tug. "I'll pray for you."

"Well," Drew said, "I need that, too. So I thank you ahead of time."

"Done," she said, and then she left.

She was back in thirty seconds, grinning. "I have to show you something. I'm wrong to take pleasure in this, but it's hard stopping myself."

Drew followed her through the kitchen and then around to the bar. He stopped in plain view of Bahar and whispered, "Oh my God."

"Hell," Mary said. She stopped right beside him.

Bahar was devouring the face of a guy Drew dreaded: Fred Vann Uncton, from Vienna by way of Santa Cruz. She had her wrists tight on his neck, fingers in his spiky black hair. She opened one eye, winked at Drew.

Fred Vann Uncton was male skank. He partied with Ritalin, and crank, and flat beer. Every girl he slept with, he bad-mouthed. He beat up guys at parties, bigger guys, little guys. He talked about knives, what he could do with them. It seemed like he never washed. Fred Vann Uncton was like a rhetorical question. He was a punchline and a verb. Among Hopkins students, his very name worked as a threat.

"Hell," Drew said louder.

"Hell!" Mary shouted. She hit Drew's arm.

The kissers separated with loud smacking noises before shifting on their stools to face Drew and Mary.

Bahar whispered something to Fred, and then Fred said, "Mary, hey what's up." His voice was like carbon monoxide. He had a long nose with a snub tip, a glossy suntan, and full red red lips. He'd squeezed into a child's-size T-shirt emblazoned with a photograph of Lil' Kim in twinkling pearl tap pants, matching heels, and a leopard print long-sleeved halter top. His arms were muscled like a horse's.

"Um, it's Fred!" Mary said. "Yo Fred."

"Like your cool shirt, Fred," Drew said. "I mean it."

"Yeah," Fred said, "it's kind of awesome. I made it."

"Wow," Drew said, "*made* it."

"Gonna lay you flat if you're making fun of me," he told Drew with a snarling smile. "Gonna do it."

"I'm not making fun of you, dude," Drew said, holding out his palms. "I know you mean business. You're a legendary thug."

Fred nodded smugly, crossed his arms over his chest.

"You're a hard-ass," Mary said.

"You too!" Fred shouted, pointing at Mary Hong. "I'll put you down, cutie perfect girl!"

"Perfect?" Bahar said. "Her?" After a moment, she smiled. "Um, Mary, I'm sorry. That was too lamely bitchy even for me. Withdrawn from the court record or whatever. Oh God, what am I saying? Like I'm falling apart before your very eyes."

Fred turned to her. "If you'd let me fuck you," he whined, "I mean I'd put you back together."

Mary turned to Drew. "You know what?" she said. "I'm leaving. Bye Fred, bye Bahar."

Bahar didn't answer. She had her cheek on Fred's shoulder. He flexed his arms for her and opened his mouth wide and shot his tongue out at Drew.

"I'll walk you," Drew said.

On the corner, in front of the lot where Mary had parked, she hugged Drew and kissed him and said, "I don't know if I can get up with you too much this summer. Do you know what I mean? That girl, I mean she's poison and I don't like the way it makes me feel."

"Fine," Drew said. "I just won't be her friend anymore. That will probably turn her attitude around."

"Drew, I mean it."

"Honey, I mean it, too. You remember me when I first got here and I was a different person?"

"I liked that person," she said. "He's not really around much anymore."

"That person was fine," Drew said. "But he was a drudge. He was such a bummer. He was like all inside myself. He was nothing. Like he was zero. Mary, I couldn't negotiate a conversation. I felt like an ugly alien and I almost dropped out of school. But Bahar came after me. I mean, it changed me. She sought me out. This beautiful girl with a way of being out here in the real world. Mary, I wouldn't be pre-med if it wasn't for her. I wouldn't have had the confident two-year run I've had in classes. Baby, I wouldn't have met you. I mean, don't you remember? She introduced us. Don't you remember how you used to be her friend, too? I've got a history with her."

Mary nodded. "I remember it very clearly."

"And I know how bad it got with you two. I understand that it got out of control."

"I couldn't take it with her. I can't. Drew, I won't."

"But I can. No one else can see it, and that's fine. But when I think about what she's done for me, there's no way I can abandon her. Mary, no one's *ever* needed me. It's probably unhealthy, but I like the feeling. I like having people who need me. Look at you. I mean, you're strong. We're friends, but you don't *need* me."

"Not like her," Mary said, and she reached into her left sock for her car keys.

"Me and Bahar like bleed into each other."

Mary turned and pointed into the parking lot with her keys. A chirp sounded from among the cars. She didn't look at Drew.

"I can't make you understand, can I?" he asked.

Mary stayed silent, looking off into the parking lot. A layer of pink exhaust sparkled in the windshields.

"What do you think?" Drew asked. "Do you think she's just all foulness? Do you like disbelieve me when I say that it's still way deep in there, somewhere, waiting, this good thing that I know? It really brought me to life, Mary. I can't walk away from her. Don't I have an obligation to my friends? If she got really sick, I mean physically sick, you wouldn't bully me into dropping her. You'd be there with me."

Mary's eyes locked on Drew's. "Let me just caution you, dude. The way I see it, you two *are* bleeding into each other. That's why I'm worried. I want you to be careful that you're not taking on more pints than she is. It matters to me. I see changes in you that maybe you don't. Where in the fuck do you think you're gonna end up? Where's she taking you? Do you have any idea?"

"Maybe I needed a dose of evil to just get me going in a good direction. When I'm a doctor, I'll save lives. So if this supposed evil chick is like an engine that powers me toward, you know, my own transformation, I accept that. I can harness that energy. I know I can."

"Allow me to say that's a chilling rationale. You could guard any loathsome act with that line."

"I love you," Drew said. He held her shoulders and kissed her forehead. "I hope you have an awesome summer."

6

When he got back, Bahar was alone at the bar, on the phone. A minute passed before Drew realized that she was talking to Ty, his little brother, down in New Orleans. He pulled onto the stool next to her; it was still warm from Fred Vann Uncton, so Drew looked up and down the bar for any signs of him. There were none.

"You wanna talk to your brother?" Bahar cooed into the phone, giving Drew her melting gaze.

It made Drew's heart hurt, just seeing inside her like this a minute after he'd called her evil. If she was evil, what was he? A lesser evil? The lesser of two evils? "Yeah," he said softly, "of course I wanna talk to my brother." As he took the phone from her, he held her finger for a moment, and he bent forward to kiss it with the inside of his lips.

"Whuddup Ty?"

"Oh, bruh, everything."

"Like what?"

"So much!"

"You're sixteen, dude. How much can be going on?"

"You can't bring me down!"

Drew pulled the phone away from his face and pointed at it.

"I *love* him more every time I talk to him," Bahar said.

"Did you hear that?" Ty blathered through the receiver. "Your friends understand me better than you do, bro."

Drew clamped it to his face. "Hey, I'm back," he said. "You'd better not nag Bahar too much."

"Can I borrow forty dollars for the weekend?"

"Um, *no*."

"Please."

"How come you need money?"

"Because I don't have any?"

"Ty."

"Android."

Drew sighed. "Okay, I'll try to figure it out. Forty bucks?"

"Thanks."

Bahar opened her purse. "I can wire Ty some dollars."

Drew put his hand over the phone mouthpiece. "You do *not* have to."

"Your brother is my brother."

"No he's not. You don't need to take on the entire Drew Burke clan—lady, my *dad* will be calling you up next, hitting up."

"Drew, it's forty dollars," she said, and shrugged.

He sat there a moment, looking into her eyes, before nodding. He told Ty, "Okay, I'll call you tomorrow morning, Western Union."

"Cool," Ty said.

"We can do it now, with my credit card, actually," Bahar said quietly. "I can handle this, Drew. Here, let me have my baby Ty."

Drew asked Ty to hold on a minute, and he pushed Hold on the bar phone. He looked hard at Bahar. "I wanna tell you something. I want you to listen to me, baby. You *better* not be getting close to that nasty whore Fred Vann Uncton. I'm not *playing* tough here. You understand me?"

"It was nothing," Bahar said, a smile turning up the corners of her mouth. "It was a coincidence. He just happened to walk in. And Gere was busy. And I was *lonely*. You *left* me to hang with all those ridiculous people: Duncan, Mary Hong. Gere got busy and I was alone and I didn't wanna be."

Drew looked at his hands. "I'm sorry. I'm *sorry*. So did Fred split?"

Bahar made a face. "I think he's back in the kitchen with um Duncan?"

"What!" Drew said.

Suddenly, one of the bathroom doors, up some stairs from the bar, flew open. Fred stepped out, grinning and glassy-eyed. He walked slowly down to Bahar and Drew, floated past them, kept his posture perfect, and drifted into the darkness of the lounge. The front door opened a moment later and afternoon light poured in.

"Bye Fred!" Bahar called daintily. "Bye darling charmer!"

"Do *not* hook up with him. I'm groveling here, I swear."

"I promise," she said.

Drew tracked down Duncan slicing limes in the kitchen: broad back in tight T-shirt, arm muscles flickering, chop chop chop. "So I had to tell you before I left that I know a lot of mad luscious chicks who would love to hook up with a tall Scot who's got those brown eyes like yours," Drew said.

Duncan paused with the knife resting on top of a lime. "Well, gulp."

Drew leaned against a tile wall. "These are smart foxy girls who die for Scottish guys. There are people who truly *pine* for an erudite Scot."

Duncan wiped his hands on his jeans and then lifted up his T-shirt to wipe his face. Drew made himself look away until the hem of the T-shirt fell back down to Duncan's lap, and the Scot held a wedge of lime up to his eye and said, "I'd like to sit around and, well, *talk* with the very pretty American girls. What do they talk about? Do they talk about Gerry Adams? Do they talk about *Trainspotting* still? How about Sylvia, our Sylvia?"

" 'The brute brute heart of a brute like you,' " Drew blurted. He had his favorite Sylvia lines, and they all came from the poem "Daddy."

Duncan looked him up and down. "Yeah, I like that one, too. I don't know if I should say this or not, but you *may* have some subconscious reason for hewing to Plath. Don't take this in the wrong way, but you *look* like her. You could be her child."

"I don't know what she looks like. What does she look like?"

Duncan leaned forward on the counter. He pressed his hands on the top so his whole upper body tensed. "She looks like a rounder, sadder you."

Drew came up next to him at the sink so their elbows barely touched. He looked straight ahead at the wall and said, "I think you have this force field around you that's just like pulling me up to you, like I'm in a satellite saucer and you're the command ship, and there are galaxies all around us, and stars."

Duncan made R2D2 noises in Drew's ear and then began to kiss his neck. The smell of lime zest was in the air. "I'd love to get up with you," he whispered.

"I have a thing going with this great guy," Drew said, but he didn't pull away from him. "I just wanna be honest about that."

Duncan took a sideways step away. "I was playing."

"That was really nice of you. I sure enjoy that."

"So you weren't teasing me?"

"My good dude is really rich," Drew said. "I'm not like sure that he's going to stick with me. Actually, I'll probably screw up the relationship. I've got a kind of chip on my shoulder. It's due to the money gap, if that's not too obvious."

"That sucks," Duncan said, and he moved back to Drew. "Hey, I hope you give me a chance to get to know you."

"Dude, if my scene falls apart, you're first on my phone list. I swear. I've had an eye on you. I'll totally take you out on some nice date. I want your phone number. Will you give it to me, man?"

"Give me yours?"

"Yeah."

"Let me get a pen," Duncan said. He bent down beside Drew and picked up his backpack. He unzipped it, stuck his hand inside, and pulled out a pen and a paperback of Sylvia Plath poems. He turned the back cover open and gave Drew the pen. "Here," he said, "just write your number here."

Drew wrote slowly, one precise number at a time, and then he signed his name. With each stroke of the pen, he thought he could hear Jake's voice, calling his name. When Drew was done, Duncan wrote out his phone number across the top of a page, tore it out and gave it to Drew.

"Look at this," Duncan said, and he flipped the book open to the center pages. He ran his thumb down the height of a tall slim photograph of the poet, and then across her face. He said, "You want to kiss me, don't ya?" He touched Drew's lips with that thumb.

"Yeah, absolutely I do," Drew said.

"Show me."

Drew looked at his shoes and shrugged. "I can't."

"Just show me with your eyes," Duncan said. "Look me right in the eyes. C'mon. Just look."

A prism turned before Drew's eyes; in every facet, he

saw the different faces: lips, Duncan's face, Sylvia's face, Duncan's lips, Sylvia's lips. Light glinted from their irises.

"Kiss me," Duncan said. " 'Tulips,' 'Cut,' 'Elm,' 'The Night Dances.' "

"The Ariel poems," Drew said. "All the death in them makes a guy feel so alive. You want to live up to your death or something, but not in a sick way. Do you know what I mean?"

Duncan nodded. " 'Berck-Plage,' " he whispered. " 'Ariel.' 'Daddy.' "

" 'Paralytic,' " Drew whispered. " 'Contusion.' "

"Kiss me," Duncan said.

Slowly, Drew obeyed.

7

Pulling onto the Route 83 ramp, Bahar started to work all the controls at once, the windows and the sunroof and the AC and the seat-tilt. When she finally had them set to her liking, she fucked around with the radio. She kept going back to the classic rock, as if she remembered the songs.

As the Eagles faded away, Drew wiped a tear from the corner of his eye and sang along, "Get you baby one of these nights . . ."

He put his palms flat on his stomach and counted slow deep deep breaths and closed his eyes. The car soared.

He saw the beach. Soft green water lapping the shore. Boats a mile out, bobbing. A foot, a girl's foot, toes digging sand. Baked seaweed across her calf.

Drew was there, touching her. He lay in a sunny stupor.

Ft. Pierce, Florida. Spring break. A couple of months ago.

They spent a week in a dilapidated fisherman's shanty, a boat tied at the dock.

Midnight, the last night, they sat on the small beach rampart and watched silver waves break. They were quiet. That's why they'd stayed friends. These silences.

They glowed from the day's sun. They were naked, salty, wet.

Drew ran his hand down the side of her face and kissed her on the lips. She kissed him back. She pulled him down on top of her.

It was the first time. It was the only time. Their knees were covered with sand that was still warm. There was just the faintest sigh off the ocean.

"Hey," Drew said, "if I'm not doing something right, will you just tell me?"

"No problem," she murmured, kissing the hollow at the base of Drew's neck. "No big deal, no big deal." She said it over and over and it was the perfect thing to say because, after a while, he got the hang of things.

To have a friend who wants to be with you and knows how to be exactly who you want her to be, who's in your arms and kissing you and holding your dick to make it bigger, who's talking low, slowly stuffing you inside her—to have that friend changed your life.

They fucked for a long time, laughing and kissing even when a stillness fell over them.

In the morning, Bahar told him that it could never happen for them, not like this. Drew looked at her beside him, his best girl, and he gave her his word. "God I love you so much I won't ever try to have sex again," he said.

"I like the sound of that," she said.

* * *

"Drew?"

He groaned, shifted in his seat, put his hands on his lap for camouflage.

"What do you wanna hear?" Bahar asked.

"Dunno," he muttered. "It's your car, honey."

She looked over at him for a moment. "I'm not that selfish, am I?"

"Nah, you're generous as all hell. I'm just sleepy all of a sudden." He let his face tip out the window, into the rush of air. The car glided above the cut-out industrial heart of the city.

Bahar switched radio stations until she found melancholy folk guitars leading a weak, sad, male voice across a desert landscape.

When the song ended, she asked, "So how would they call for a horse if it didn't have a name?"

"Hmmm," Drew said. "Good question." He breathed loudly before settling back in his seat. There was no way that shrinks knew that the drugs they prescribed could make you feel so good, so peaceful as you watched out the windows.

The car slid lightly over the black road. Trees passed. Brown utility poles wavered in procession.

It felt good to be heading to Bahar's secluded old pink brick farmhouse on a woodsy stretch of road. It felt good to breathe the clean air.

You felt like you owned the breeze, like you owned the trees.

You had your own orchard. You had your own pond, your own hot spring, your own stream, your own mill. You had a Jaguar and a Volvo and a Legend and a silver Range Rover.

Drew crinkled his eyes open and looked over at Bahar.

How come you have everything?

How come you take it so for granted?

He nudged his face out the window again, let the wind soothe. He fell into a mood of hypnotized entitlement, as if he owned this highway and the blue-black clone sedans in every lane were part of a security detail that was escorting him home.

Through suburban Maryland the highway was wide, eight lanes, double-wide exit ramps, traffic throbbing north at eighty pushing eighty-five. The sky turned the color of a night-time ocean, and into Pennsylvania the horse farms and crop fields rolled all the way to the horizon. Toward York, the distant hills were clay-red. Lakes were blue disks dotted with dusk-fisher skiffs. By the time they crossed the Lancaster County line, the highway was just two lanes in each direction, separated by wildflower fields.

It wasn't spring anymore, Drew noticed. It was true summer. Sloping away from the highway were dark fields of ankle-high corn and tobacco: family farms. The clear green smells and dark leaves and *whoosh-whoosh* highway quiet fixed him in a vulnerable mood.

Without asking, he turned down the radio.

Suddenly, the farms and houses and power lines and billboards, all of it, whipped past them.

Drew loved to fly like this and Bahar knew it. He loved going ninety, ninety-five, smooth on the old road. Bahar drove calmly and happily, cutting traffic. Headlights were like stars on the glass.

When she finally slowed down, it was like the Legend glided in reverse to meet the pack of slower cars—a jet landing. Drew looked over at her, grinning.

The engine clicked down to a soft pulse as Bahar turned onto Marietta Avenue, away from Lancaster city, past trim subdivisions rising out of the woods, past two dark empty roadside farm stands. The car picked up speed once they hit wide open countryside. They rose up a tipping-down hill aglow with stars and fireflies.

At the third rural intersection, they turned left on a narrow road, crossed a covered bridge, made a sharp left on Bahar's road.

Drew sat up at attention because he loved the approach to her fortress.

Stones popped under the car tires. Low-hanging leaves smacked the windshield and roof. The air smelled like cut grass. They fell through one stand of trees into the moonlight only to come upon an even thicker barrier of leaves and branches sagging from above.

Bahar crept through them. When she broke free, she zoomed the length of the stone driveway and killed the engine.

The house sat back against a screen of pines. It was pink-red brick, scraped raw. It was three stories. Every curtain was drawn.

"We're home," Bahar said, and popped open their door locks.

Drew nodded. He stood out of the car. He stretched and took a couple of steps toward the house before a blue-white light came on with a silent pop. Security. A smaller red bulb flashed in the zip window above the side door.

Bahar pointed her keychain at the house, running her thumb on the edge until the light went off. She hip-shoved her car door and it clicked shut. She marched to the front door. Her earrings, her necklace, the rings on her fingers and the highlights in her hair, all of it—everything sparkled in the dark.

8

She keyed in the alarm-disable code. Drew came in right after her. She flicked on the lights.

They stood on a polished pine floor in a long room with wide, deep fireplaces and a wet bar that ran the length of the opposite wall. One stretched-out plump sofa sat in the center, on a frayed Amish quilt, and in the corner there was a lab-quality stereo and big-screen TV.

"I'm hungry again," Bahar said, and started toward the ground-floor kitchen. Her sandals clacked across the floor. "Could ya eat something?"

"Maybe," Drew said.

"Find some music. Get yourself a beer."

"Done."

He went to the bar and snicked two Red Stripes before he spun the dial to find a Fleetwood Mac revival. He hit a switch to bring all the speakers to life, and suddenly every room boomed with "Ooh always/been a storm . . ."

He found Bahar singing along in clear voice with Stevie Nicks as she carried bowls and plates and pint containers to the fat fir table built into the bay window. It looked out over Redder's Road, the tumbledown stone mill, and the white-capped stream surging over the dam. Last summer, Drew remembered, he and Bahar pretended they were eco-racers, and climbed up the dam, daring each other to go faster, to scale the stones more recklessly.

He hung over the cold food and plucked a medallion of lobster from its oily bowl.

"Candles?" Bahar asked, sliding next to him so her cheek just barely brushed his.

"Yeah," he said, pinching a firm wet wedge of pineapple.

As he walked away, she patted his ass.

He came back clutching two blue pillar candles. Bahar lit them, sat down, motioned for Drew to sit. She piled salad on their plates. They took turns with bowls and plates of lobster meat, and grilled red potatoes, and Bing cherries, and poached salmon. After he sucked down the two Red Stripes, Drew helped Bahar drink the pitcher of iced tea. For dessert, they moved to the window seat at the end of the table, munched fudge-covered Oreos. He kept a free hand in her lap, and every now and then he'd run his hand down the front of her thigh.

Drew gazed out at the mill, the silver traces in the stream.

"I'm going to go for a quick swim," Bahar said after a while. "You wanna come?"

"In a minute," he said.

She leaned over to kiss him. She closed her eyes, but he kept his open to watch her lovely face. She wore an ashen plum lipstick, and the flickering candlelight dusted her cheeks like powder. This was his best friend, he told himself. This imperfect, loving girl. A friend for life.

9

The phone rang. Drew snatched it off the wall. "Hello?"

"It's Arnie."

"Hey Arnie. Bahar's doing laps."

"I like that pool they have there."

"Yup."

"That's a nice house."

"Swank," Drew said.

Arnie's voice dropped conspiratorially. "I could live there."

"Yeah," Drew said.

"Couldn't you see me living there?"

"Um, maybe," he said noncommittally.

"Well, anyway, can you give her a message?"

"Yeah."

"Tell her I'm finishing up that brief, so I might not make it until tomorrow morning. I'm gonna try for tonight, but

I'm not one hundred percent. She can call me at the office if she wants to."

"Aw, she's gonna be sad," Drew said.

"You'll keep her company, right?"

As soon as Drew hung up, the phone rang again. He picked up.

"It's you, thank goodness, Drew," Bahar's mother, Tamar, said breathlessly. Glass and silver tinkled behind her voice.

"You guys eating?"

"We're seated," she answered. "Is Bahar around?"

"She's swimming."

"How about Jake?"

"No."

"Good," she said. "I have something to ask you."

"Yeah," Drew said. "What's up?"

"You know how hard I work?"

"Yeah."

"But do you know why?" Something was changing in her voice. A note of desperation had crept in.

"Because you like the work?" Drew said.

"No no no no no. I don't like this, Drew. I don't like to go on *Larry King*. I mean that."

"Oh."

"It's to build a wall, Drew. I have to build a wall."

"Oh."

"Have you ever built a wall to keep out the bad, Drew?"

"Well," he said, "I don't know."

"Oh, you'd know. You'd definitely know."

"Okay."

"Look," she said with a sudden breeziness, "I just wanted to tell you, well, that Jake absolutely loves you. I mean that, Drew. I don't want you to have any doubt about that."

Drew smiled into the phone. "Thank you for saying that. But I don't like know what to say, actually."

"That's the beauty of it," she said. "You can say anything, I think. And he'll still love you that much." She paused a moment to drag on a cigarette and then she chuckled. "Christ, I'm embarrassing myself. Drew, you don't mind if I hang up now, do you honey? I should go. This old gal's getting soft."

"No," Drew said. "You have a good night."

Right before she disconnected, Tamar murmured, "Listen to him, Drew. Please."

"Goodnight," he said, and clicked the phone off. He looked at it and wondered what she meant.

10

Drew lay on a chaise lounge, drying off after his quick swim, working on a fresh beer. His warm buzz had fixed him in a mood of gentle contemplation.

As Bahar pulled herself up the pool ladder, pale green water lapped up the sides, spilled over. She stood dripping on the tile apron. Drew watched between her legs: pool water settling to calm polar-cap blue, underwater light drawing white spirals across the sides and bottom, taut rope stretching down the center to make lanes.

Bahar turned around, flicking her hair; the long, ropy, brown strands spiraled in the air, and in Drew's vision they fused with the landscape behind her, across the water. Rows of gnarled pines grew up a sharp hill; where the incline plateaued, trees grew for acres.

She shook water from her ear and then she reclined, regally, on the lounge beside him. Water pooled along her thighs on the firm black cushion. She took a sip of iced tea.

Drew finished his beer. They were quiet for a long while in the hush of countryside night. Drew closed his eyes and let the thrumming pool filter and rushing treetops soothe him. He counted his breaths up to ten and then back down to one, thumbing his temples, listening to the way his pulse slowed.

"Arnie called," he said after a while.

"He's not coming, is he?"

"Yeah," Drew said, "he's coming. Maybe late tonight, or like maybe not till tomorrow morning."

"I have to talk to him."

"I know you do. Late tonight or tomorrow."

"Okay."

"And your mom called. To tell me how much Jake loves me. That I should listen to him."

Bahar chuckled uneasily. "My dear dear Tamar. Don't let mommy get to you."

"I won't," he said lightly.

"Okay," she murmured.

Drew looked out at the trees, out at the first layer of thin branches. A trace of panic cut through him. "Hey, what was that?" he asked, jerking up in his seat.

Something white and round, like a face, had shown for just a moment in the branches. It was gone now, subtracted.

Bahar grabbed his arm. "What do you think you saw?"

"I don't know," he said, but his blood pumped cold. "It went away so quick."

"Oh, an *owl*, probably," she prompted him. "It's ghoulish how they look when they fly off."

"I don't know," he said again, his voice trailing off. He peered out into the trees, surveying each blue-black space between shiny dark leaves. "I don't know how it could have been an owl. It just fit right there in the branches."

"Drew, it was nothing. You're scaring me a little bit."

He turned to look at her. "Okay," he said, "it was nothing."

"Well, it was nothing to worry about," she said. "You're too nervous, baby."

"You know, on that subject," Drew started. He winced, put an open hand on his forehead. "I have to tell you something."

"Is this about Duncan?"

Drew nodded.

"I wondered." She palmed her belly.

"I had a moment with Duncan that I shouldn't have had. It was a moment when our like emotional tectonic plates shifted before us and we were helpless to stop. Do you know what I mean?"

Bahar was impassive. "Just tell me the whole story, baby. And then I'll know what you mean."

"Well, we were just hanging out in the kitchen, and I quoted a line of Sylvia Plath, and then he told me I reminded him of her, a happier version of her, and he kept saying it like he knew her, as if he'd met her, as if he'd just gotten off the phone with her. It was a dark thing in my eyes, he said. It was the way I pronounce a couple of words, he said. You know, it's the kind of thing any guy would laugh off. It's a come-on. It's the smoothie-woothie.

But it didn't even occur to me, then, to laugh it off. Then he rubbed his thumb across my eyebrows, slow slow slow, and then down my nose. I got turned out, Bahar. He put the tip of his thumb in my mouth and he quoted the poem about the moon, the moon dragging the ocean all over the place, the moon is bald and the moon is wild and the moon is no door. Bahar, it made feelings rise to the surface, like here on the surface of my skin—" He stopped and roughly massaged his chest and belly. "My blood hurt inside me. My aorta pinched like I was going to die, but what did I care if I died."

Just then, a car door slammed out front. It had to be Jake.

"Ah!" Bahar blurted, eyes wide open, looking over at Drew.

Surprising himself, he stayed calm. "But all I did was kiss."

"Jake won't understand that."

"I think he will."

"Well, I'm your tomb," Bahar said. "Not a word."

"I know," Drew said. "I know the real you."

He lifted his face until his chin pointed at the stars. Like strung lights, they blinked.

11

Jake came around the side of the house in a white dress shirt that glimmered in the dark. He walked long confident strides, keys jangling in his pocket. He carried a six-pack in one hand and with the other he unfastened his belt buckle.

"O's won," he called out. "I feel good. I want somebody to be mine. Is there someone here who'll be mine?"

Sparks notched up Drew's legs.

"How are *mein* people?" Jake asked, whipping the belt free of its final loop. "*Mein* mighty sister, *mein* strong fine friend Drew? How's it feel to be you two?"

"We're fine," Bahar and Drew said in almost glum unison.

Jake kissed Bahar first, and she said, "What in the shit are you doing with fresh beer?"

"I'm *drinking*," he said. He dropped onto her chair, one thigh banging on her stomach.

Drew winced but didn't say anything.

"No you're not," she said, and grabbed at the six pack.

He held his arm up over her, cans dangling. "Bahar, I'm going to have a beer or two. Take it up with my counsel here." He jabbed her belly with stiff fingers.

Drew rose up in his seat with a cry. "Jake, leave her alone. Don't do that."

"*Never* do that again," she cried, and pushed at his shoulder. "This is just the perfect night to drop a year of sobriety. Jesus. And don't you ever ever ever poke me like that." She massaged her middle with the palm of her hand.

"Yeah, don't do that," Drew joined in.

"Okay, deal closed, men." Jake's eyes locked on Drew's, and it was like flame licked out the corners of his sockets. He rose from Bahar's lap, came around to Drew, sat on the chaise with his thigh pressed to Drew's thigh. He put his hand on Drew's damp swim suit. He bent down to open his mouth on Drew's for a rough stubbly kiss, clicking teeth. The way he leaned on Drew made it hard, hard to breathe deep, but it felt good to have that weight on his chest and it felt good to be held.

"You put up with our shit the way not one other person would. Doesn't he put up with our shit, Bahar? Isn't he our kindly gentle savior?"

She didn't answer. She sat forward, elbows on knees, looking out at the black woods.

The air had chilled. A light vapor rose off the pool.

"So what was the score?" Drew asked. He bit on Jake's lip.

"Nine to four." Jake slurped on Drew's tongue.

"And how'd Brady do?"

"Triple in the second, couple walks, sacrifice fly." Jake let his hand slip down Drew's stomach, started to mess with the waist of his bathing suit. He put the tip of his thumb in Drew's belly button. Then he stopped. "What's on your neck, dude?"

"Nice stick Brady hits with," Drew said. "What's he batting?"

"No, I asked you what's that on your neck. Looks like—yup, it looks like my boyfriend's got a hickey."

"Well kids," Bahar said, getting up from her seat, "I'm gonna step inside."

"Oh, you should hang out with us for a while," Drew said. "If you don't mind."

Jake put his hand flat on Drew's chest and pressed him to the chaise. "Bahar, we've got the whole weekend to hang out. Why don't you leave us?"

"I've heard of free will, too, brother," she said, and gave a wink to Drew. "I've been enlightened. I'm going in." She bunched a hand and kissed her fingers, waved to him. "Don't do anything *else* stupid, sweetie."

"Was she talking to me?" Drew asked, and he tried to lift up. Jake held him down. "Who gave you a hickey?"

"It was just something stupid," Drew said. "I swear to God it was nothing."

Jake pulled back his fist, as if to play punch. "I'll flatten your nose if you don't tell me the truth."

Drew tried to sit up, but Jake pushed him back down. "This is a bad sign, man," Drew said.

"Well, yeah, it sure is." His fingers crawled up Drew's neck, traced the circumference of the hickey. "Why would you do this? Is there something you can't get from *me*?" He stretched out on top of Drew, lay his forehead on Drew's. "I'm not gonna let you go 'til I get an answer. I mean, I'll smother you." His fingers tightened on Drew's neck—at first with gentle force, like he was looking for a pulse, but then they pushed harder up into Drew's jawline. There was something raw in Jake's voice as he slipped his lips to Drew's ear and whispered, "I won't let you do that to us."

"Let go," Drew rasped, and right away Jake did, murmuring his soft apology. *What the hell?*

Drew closed his eyes for a moment. When he opened them, sighing, all he could see was Jake's face hovering over him, blocking the sky. "I had a couple of drinks this afternoon and I kissed the bartender a while. It was all my fault. It was retarded of me. I'm sorry."

"Did you mean it?" Jake asked. His breath was beery, hot. The thing was, he'd been in AA for as long as Drew knew him, went to a meeting maybe once a week, but he also had the periodic beer, just one or two. A secret. A secret that Bahar, Queen of Sober, didn't know.

"Did you mean it with the bartender?" Jake asked again.

"Mean what?"

"When you kissed him?"

Drew was silent. He looked to the side, where Jake's big hand gripped the chair.

Jake patted the side of his cheek, a sharp chop. "Why would I let you just screw around with anyone you wanted to? How would you know that I love you?" He hit Drew's cheek a little bit harder.

"It was so fucking stupid of me," Drew said. "I'm sorry."

"Tell me it'll never happen again."

"It'll never happen again."

"Tell me you'd rather kill yourself than hurt me like that."

Drew shifted beneath him. "I would never say that. I won't say that, Jake."

"Fine. Then I will. *I'd* rather you kill yourself than hurt us like that."

Bahar's voice came out a window. "You okay, Drew? You need me to call 911?"

"He's fine," Jake said. "I just put the gag in his mouth. Did you get the kerosene?"

"Drew?" Bahar asked, a pang in her voice.

"Well," Jake said, looking deep into Drew's eyes, "I'm going to let you go. I'm going to be cool to you."

"I'm okay," Drew called out.

"Fuck yeah you're okay," Jake said. "I love you, you know."

Drew lifted his shoulders off the chaise. Jake's hand slid to his lap. "I wasn't scared of you," Drew said.

Jake grinned. "Yes you were."

The way Jake kissed him, it was like he wanted to fit

all of Drew inside his mouth. First he'd eat his head, and then he would lick clean the rest of Drew. He'd break the bones over his knees; black blood would pool at his feet. And then Drew would be gone.

Jake kissed Drew with his tongue fat in his mouth, like a hand. He held Drew crushed against him, his hard thumb pressing, pressing Drew's nipple like he wanted to shove it into his heart.

Jake whimpered, kissing him, like weeks had passed, like it was the last time that they would ever kiss. No one had ever wanted to kiss Drew like this. No one had ever wanted to kiss him until it hurt.

Drew pulled his hand out of Jake's grip and wiped tears from his own cheeks. He stopped kissing. His lips slid down Jake's wet chin. Jake licked the bridge of his nose, his whole body shaking as if a motor had broken loose in his chest.

"Why are you like this?" Drew asked.

Jake opened his mouth, but no words came out.

"Boy, when you're like this is when it's scary," Drew said.

"I can't *stop* myself," Jake finally whispered.

"You're like storms," Drew whispered back. "You're a weather system."

"I'm *your* weather, man," Jake said. "Let *me* tell *you* about a wind."

Drew nodded. He could feel his blood pumping redder.

Something black shifted inside Drew. He pulled away from Jake. The air between them crackled. Jake winced like a fist had just grazed his cheek, and then he tried to pull Drew up against him again.

"So how was work?" Drew asked desperately. Normally, when he first got home, Jake liked to talk about work and school. He majored in architecture at Franklin & Marshall College and worked fifty hours a week on building sites around the county, unpaid.

It was time, Drew thought, for a mellow moment.

"Who *cares*?" Jake asked. "I don't wanna talk about that."

"I want to talk for a minute," Drew said. "Let's just exist."

Again, Jake winced. He slowly brought his hand out of Drew's bathing suit and brought it up to his nose. He sniffed loudly and then he licked the fingers.

"C'mon," Drew said. "How was work?"

Jake took a deep breath. "Harsh," he answered. "Work was too harsh today." Then he smiled with his big open mouth. "But I sure was up to the challenge." His neck and shoulders relented. "There were shitstorms all day. Actually, it was a good work day. It was distracting."

"Hey, so tell me what went on, man."

Jake laughed to himself and then reached over to tweak Drew's nose. "Like the Amish were unhappy today. The trusses were *all* for shit, a foot off here, a foot too wide there, and so on. When a guy wants to put up forty houses, he needs trusses at a precise moment in time and he needs them properly engineered. It was like mayhem. But I felt like I was part of it. I felt like God couldn't lift me out of there without messing up the whole operation. That was good to feel."

"So did you threaten to punch the guys at the truss mill?"

Jake shook his head. "I wasn't going to actually hit you," he beseeched. "C'mon."

Drew faked a right cross to the side of Jake's head, and then they touched fists as if at the start of a bout.

"I'm *alive* because of you and that's the truth," Jake stated. "That's how it feels to me." He dropped his arms and fell heavily toward Drew. "If I hadn't met you I'd be dead by now. I would have killed myself. That's how it's been for years. I've been wanting a rope around my neck."

"Dude," Drew said softly. "I'm not anyone special. You're the strong guy whether I'm here or not. Don't be so dark. Don't be sad tonight. I'm not special."

"No," Jake moaned. "You accept me, man. You make me feel like I can live."

"Why so heavy *tonight*? I'm sorry for the bartender. It didn't mean anything."

Jake closed his eyes, didn't answer. Drew let him brood.

A fistful of broad green leaves fell off branches and landed in the pool. They skated toward the deep-end skimmer hole. The cooling winds picked up. Goose flesh rose up Drew's legs.

"You're okay, Teddy Roosevelt," Drew said. "C'mon. C'mon." He massaged the back of Jake's neck.

"I don't want to be the sad guy. I hate it. But I need you."

"That's not who I think you are. And I'm right here." Pulling Jake's collar back, he started to rub his shoulders.

Jake sighed a deep whoosh and fell back toward Drew. His dark scent rose in the air. He reached back for Drew's leg. "I feel sad when I'm away from you."

"I'm right here," Drew said quietly.

"But you're gonna leave, and that makes me so fucking furious at you, and I know that's not fair. How come I only see you on the weekend? You're an hour and a half away. I should see you more. It shouldn't be just the weekends."

Drew held him. "I don't want to fight you. I want to kiss you and shit."

Jake's face lifted up toward him and they kissed. Drew felt the atoms that made up his cheeks and his chin flicker. He pulled on the tail of Jake's shirt.

"Hey," Jake said, pointing past the pool where the ascending hill of trees glowed darkly, "let's go up there. I want to get up with you, okay?" His voice was wet with sadness. "That's gonna be the only thing to lift me."

Drew followed the line from Jake's finger, out into the deep woods. For a moment, a trick of the light, he thought he caught a glimpse of the round white face. But that was just being a pussy.

He lifted Jake's shirt up his back and kissed the cleft. He whispered, "Yeah, I wanna do that. Let's go."

Jake lifted up from him and stepped off the chair. He pulled off his shirt. He had the shoe-polish brown skin, black fuzz the width and down the flat belly. He stepped out of his pants, threw them on Drew, and just stood there in white boxers, waiting, near-panting with not only lust but that desperate heavy weight of fury and fear.

It worked on Drew. It got him up out of the lounge chair, got his hand on Jake's ass. He took the lead. He guided Jake through a dark opening in the branches. There was no trail that he could see.

12

Drew sat on the dirt floor of the woods, pulling his bathing suit on. "Teddy Roosevelt, that was dedicated," he said, and then he lay back and watched Jake, standing over him, slide boxers up his thick legs. The moon and the pool lights shined dimly through the thick mesh of pine branches.

Jake rested his foot on Drew's knee and pushed it down to the ground. "I could devour you, man. I mean, if we could ever get far past the laughing."

Drew smiled. "That's something you just *got* to accept. I can try to not laugh, but there's a lot about sex that is so retarded. Just because I don't like treat it as a sacrament doesn't mean I'm not, you know, being immolated or whatever."

"But sometimes it feels like you're making fun of me."

"Look," Drew said, "I mean *look*. I'm sitting down here, you know, at your fucking *feet*. Jake, you are so good—I mean, I think it feels so great. But do I have to take on like a persona so you believe me?"

"But it sounds like you're saying it ironically."

"I'm not," Drew protested, almost laughing. "Do I have like a drawl? Is that what it is?" He put his hands over his face. "Shit, do I have to take voice lessons so I sound less ironic so you believe me when I say I dig you and I dig having sex with you?"

"Maybe if you said it in Spanish?"

"I'm not saying it in Spanish. That's not my language."

"Say it in Dutch."

"Nah."

"German."

"Nope."

"Then just say it in English again."

"I dig you."

"Thank you. I dig back."

Drew ran his fingers up Jake's leg. "Yeah, yeah." He rested his other hand on top of Jake's foot and thumbed the contours of his toes. Then he noticed the scars between the toes. In the dark, he couldn't see them, but he could feel the nubby slickness. The scars were cold.

Jake made a nervous sound in his throat and pulled away.

"Where you going?" Drew asked.

"I wanna swim some laps."

"Oh."

"What's the matter?"

"Nothing's the matter. I mean, go swim."

Jake squatted down beside him, ran the back of his hand down Drew's cheek. "I don't want you to take this the wrong way, but you shouldn't sulk like a little boy. You can't be a little boy and a man at the same time. A man doesn't pout."

Drew tried to swallow, but his throat didn't work.

"Don't take shit from me," Jake said, and he started to tap Drew's chest with two fingers. "Show me I can't run over you."

Drew's heart took two strong cold beats high up in his chest. He heard instinctual voices sort of chanting in his head, but they were all running together, and his body wouldn't move in response.

Jake took him by the shoulders and pushed him to the ground and held him there tight. He said, "I want you to fight back."

"Jake," Drew said evenly, "get off me."

"*Fight* back. I want to see you fight back."

Drew asked him again, but Jake pressed down on him even harder and murmured, "I know this guy, there was this guy, I thought he was my friend but he wasn't my friend, he was so weak . . ."

"Who are you talking about?"

"It's the past," Jake said in a tight voice.

Drew was silent for a while, and he felt red shame start to settle over him, but then, in a quiet voice, he said, "Whatever you think you know about me, you're wrong.

If you don't get off me, I'll break something, part of your body, even if I end up worse off than you."

Jake smiled and let him go. "That's all I wanted to hear." As he started to rise up, he pressed his hand down on Drew's stomach for support and pushed down hard, so it hurt, and that was all it took for Drew to flinch and then roar to his knees and tackle Jake headfirst to the ground. He landed heavy on Jake's back, driving an elbow against his spine. He pushed Jake's face into a puddle of leaves and tucked his knees up high on Jake's shoulders to pin him there.

"You did this to me," Drew said, shaking his head. "Why? Just for some fun? Man, you can piss a guy off."

Jake got his face out of the leaves and sucked in a mouthful of air. Then he started laughing.

"You can't laugh at me," Drew said, pushing his knees hard on top of Jake.

"I don't know why." Jake laughed. "You got me, dude. I can't move."

"Yeah, you can't," Drew said, and something inside him began to relent.

"Now I'm getting to know you," Jake said. "Now I know you're solid."

"What do you mean? What are you talking about?"

"I know you're solid."

"What's that—a compliment? You're not going to beat up on me all the time. Like I have a little brother, dude. I know how to fight. But why does that matter to you tonight?"

"It just does. It matters to me that you're strong."

"Don't compliment me. That pisses me off."

Jake made a small ooh of pain and shifted beneath Drew. "No, it's just the fucking truth. I need to know what kind of man you are. I'm counting on you. You have no idea how much I'm counting on you. I want you to be here. I want you to get through this all in one piece. You have to."

Would it always be like tonight? Was this how it would always feel to love Jake? Would there always be a welling-up chaotic fear that could sweep you away with it? Drew didn't know if even at his strongest he was enough ballast for this storm-tossed Jake.

"You'll be here, won't you?" Jake asked.

"What does that mean? Be here when? I want to understand. Jake, what the fuck are you talking about?"

"Nothing," Jake murmured in the back of his throat. "Nada."

Drew helped Jake to his feet and they started down the trail to the pool.

"Tell me what you did today at *your* work," Jake said.

Drew turned around to face him and said, "In case you can't see me clearly, that's my 'you-must-be-crazy' look."

"Don't sulk."

Drew sort of laughed and pushed past branches into the backyard. "I guess I won't." He stopped and looked up at the back of the house, all lighted up so the pool glimmered with circles of white and gold. Stars drifted. Leaves rolled in the warm night breeze. "I proofread some pamphlets and

I researched an argument about taxes. That was my workday."

Jake put his hand on Drew's back and massaged the wing muscles until Drew sighed, all the time murmuring, "Tell me more, tell me more."

"It was just work."

"Tell me about your boss."

"You *know* who Matt Lassman is. Doesn't your *mom* know him?"

"He's how old?"

"Thirty-five, thirty-six."

"That's where I see myself at his age. Like CEO."

"Yeah, you're a big shot."

Jake's hand came around front and started to trace Drew's nipple. "Is Matt Lassman taking a mentor interest in you? Is he gonna develop your career? You're not too young to have a mentor. I mean especially since your dad is like—"

"Teddy Roosevelt needs to quit talking about my damn fatherlessness. You and Bahar both."

"I'm thinking about *our* future. Forget my sister."

"I'm going to med school. Why do I need to court Matt Lassman this week?"

"Because he's a thirty-five-year-old CEO. Court him for me."

Drew was quiet for a minute, digesting, and then he nodded. "I'll do it for you, if I can figure out how not to be obvious."

"That's what I like to hear. Friend, we're going to be a

duo. I mean, it is *written*." Jake walked around Drew, and when he got to the lip of the pool he dove in backward: a high arc, splash, and he was swallowed by the white-blue water. His dark form pulsed to the far corner. He burst out of the water, shaking the wet from his hair and face. "Hurry up," he called, hitching himself on the edge and lifting up so he sat with shins and feet dangling in the water. "Come to Teddy."

Drew looked over at the house and saw Bahar's shadow pass in front of the dining room window. His instinct pulled him to join her inside and just talk, go to sleep early on clean sheets. He could sleep for a week. A month. He stood still for a while, looking across the water at Jake. His spirit ticked up his spine and finally floated up above him, urging him to just fucking move. "Okay," he said, and took a running leap into the pool. He swam the length and came up for air between Jake's legs.

13

Drew turned a lap, tapping the tile wall, and then stretched out at the bottom of the pool. This big hushed blackness was like dying. The opaline white light in the deep-end wall pulled him toward it. He writhed in its direction, a coil of warm water.

Suddenly, bubbles streamed away from the light. There was an overpowering noise, a churning.

Jake thundered toward him, overhead, with long even strokes. Drew lay on his back, watching, as his legs kicked past.

Drew floated up to the side, pushed out of the pool, caped a towel over his shoulders, and stood there watching Jake swim. The rhythm and repetition, just the act of moving, always made Drew's body relax. When he watched hard drills, it was like he entered a deep, quiet hole in his brain. His thoughts untangled.

He was a thousand miles from home. He'd left his mom

and his brother far behind. He was like the man who struck out on his own, to work in a stronger economy, to work where there was work to do and send money back home to colonial Louisiana. For now, he could only send leftover student-loan money, a thousand bucks two times a year. But this road was long. And he could convince himself, no problem, that he *was* going to get through med school, be a doctor making dollars, let his mom retire, buy her a house, a new car, a masseuse, and a good shrink. Whatever it took to make her happier.

He wanted enough money to buy his father off, too. Just one check, a reasonable amount. But with the condition that Dad never contacted him again.

He missed his brother most of all. He wanted to be home like a bitch, watch a soccer game. He wanted to see the grass, lights, tailgates, fireflies, the white ball clouding past and Ty chasing it with that crazy virtuoso bragging lung-power.

Ty's face, running toward him as the crowd cheered, became a white ball, and then it became the round white pool light. Milky, lapping water melted the light until its pale circumference was all Drew could see.

He blinked. Jake swam below him without sign of weariness.

"I'm going inside!" Drew called. "I'll see you inside. Wake me up if I fall asleep."

Mid-stroke, Jake held his fingers in a peace V, up out of the water.

* * *

Drew walked into the house and called for Bahar.

No answer.

He passed through the empty kitchen and stopped at the bottom of the stairs, called up, but still there was no answer.

He walked down the center hallway, peering in each room until his ear caught a faint throbbing melody. Taking it slow, he padded into the dining room, where he saw the light. He ducked past a low narrow archway into an alcove full of family furnishings: scuffed pine hutches and endtables, high cabinets overflowing with linens, maps, faded board games, outdated alarm clocks, answering machines and computers. In the corner, an old shelf stereo played softly, a devout, hungry Algerian drum-and-chant.

Bahar lay stretched out on the long grandmotherly olive sofa, in panties and bra, feet buried beneath cushions. Drew came behind her, almost whispering her name. It was dark except for the stereo and the wan dining-room flicker, so he wasn't sure that she saw him. He hovered up to the sofa, but just as he was about to touch her he saw that she was on the phone—a palm-sized cell pressed to her cheek. A tiny green light glowed on her teeth.

The whites of her eyes shifted, registered his presence. His eyes adjusted to the dark, and he saw her give him a stay-with-me nod. Her whites rested on him. She listened to the phone voice in her hand.

The quiet crackled and dragged on. Shadows hung like bats in the corners. Drew shifted on his feet. He reached out to lay his hand on her shoulder, but then he pulled back.

After a minute, he leaned over the sofa and whispered, "I'll be right out there in the dining room."

She nodded, smiling her green teeth.

He sat at the dining-room table, beneath the weak chandelier of pale, sparking bulbs reflecting like spider eyes in each tear-shaped bit of dangling glass. The beer and the Ativan and the sex and the swimming had filled him with the sweetest kind of apathy. He could sit in this hard chair forever.

But it wasn't long before Bahar called for him.

He ducked back into the alcove.

"So what's up with Arnie?"

"Oh," she said. "We fought. He's not coming. He doesn't want a baby. But what do I care? I'll just have it on my own. You'll help, right?"

"Mmmm," he murmured.

"What?" Bahar said.

"Of course I'll help," Drew said. "But first you have to get the doctor's verdict, right?"

"Mmm-hmm," she murmured, and put a pillow on her face. After a moment, she flipped over onto her stomach, kicking her legs.

Drew's eyes lingered on the perfect skin of Bahar's legs, the backside where they smoothed out from black panties. As he watched that still, soft flesh, his dick started to ache. He put his palm on the back of her knee, that tender skin, and the contact sparked. He thought he could hear what she wanted from him, thought he could hear her brain making words she wouldn't say out loud. She wanted comfort, he thought, she wanted solace. Maybe a back rub, maybe just a soft kiss on her bare back. He inched his body closer, on his knees, and then he closed his eyes, trying to be instinctual. He hovered there, blind for a long ticking moment. He fell forward, his open mouth fell forward and landed, wet, on the back of her thigh, and for a moment he was just stuck there as if his lips had frozen to her skin, but then his mouth got juicier and started to slide, and he slipped inch by inch up her taut hard smooth thigh. He could smell her and he wanted to nudge deeper, up into the cleft between her legs, such a sleek pouch beneath such a narrow strip of fabric, the panties hugging the curve of her ass, and before he knew it he had his hands beside his mouth, gently pushing her legs open, and he licked up into the ridge, the cheek peeking out of her bikini bottom, kissing her, smelling her, and he took a soft bite of the slick fabric and pulled it sloppily away from her skin.

She lay perfectly still, murmuring.

He let the fabric slip from his mouth, and it snapped down on her skin.

"That's enough," she said softly.

"Okay. I know."

"Drew," she said, turning her mouth away from the pillow. "I *am* pregnant. I've known all week. I just wasn't ready to share it with you."

"Oh," he said carefully. He didn't want to set her off.

"I'm relieved you're telling me now." He leaned his face closer. Somehow, he thought he'd be more surprised. "And I mean—you're like happy?"

She twisted onto her side, smiled at him. "Yes I'm happy."

"Is it—is it *Arnie's*? But you guys have been together for like a month?"

"Yeah," she blurted. "For about a month. We met just after Florida. Arnie doesn't want to be a dad."

"Florida," Drew said. "I didn't wear a rubber in Florida."

"I know."

"How do we deal with that?"

"I don't know," she said. She sat up to face him, somber. "I don't know."

Drew pawed and elbowed her legs open so he was talking to her belly. He palmed it. Softly, he said, "I'm fucking *how* touched that you're sharing this with me." He looked up into her eyes, smiling, and said, "Hey, at the very least I'm gonna get to know a baby. I love that. I'll take the dad role whenever you'd like me to. Like weekends, nights, whenever. I mean, I'll do it as often as you want me to. I swear. Screw Arnie. Maybe he's not even the dad. Bahar, maybe I am."

She blinked her eyes slowly. Drew could see the wet light and the glistening cheeks. "I might *have* to marry you," she said. "Not a terrible way to spend our lives, is it?"

"No," Drew cooed.

"And I've been thinking, either way, if it's a boy or a girl, no matter what, I'm naming it after you."

Drew slipped up her body. He closed his mouth on her mouth. A clock chimed. Her tongue slipped past his lips.

He opened his eyes in surprise and made a little gasp. Their teeth clicked. Her breath tasted grassy.

Just as quickly, she pulled her lips away. She left him panting.

"Oh," Drew said.

"Hell if that should've just happened," she said. Getting up from the couch, she stubbed her toe. "Damn it!" She hopped a jaggy line under the archway, out to the dining room.

"Bahar," Drew called.

"I'm going," she said. "I need to go for a drive."

"No. Don't go. You can't just walk out on me like this."

She turned around in the dining room to look back at him. She picked her foot up in her hand and massaged the stubbed toe. "What are you gonna do about it?" she asked with sudden severity.

"I'm going to stop you," he said softly. "I won't let you go away."

As he lurched up from the sofa, it was like he'd torn a thick hole in the air. Bahar had herself propped in the archway. She let go with a soaked, piercing scream.

Drew stopped in place.

A ferocious silence hung in the air.

"What are you doing?" he said, and sat down hard on the sofa.

"I'm not worth your pity," she said. "Keep it to yourself. It might just kill me. I'm begging you. Keep your pity to yourself."

"That's not what I was feeling," he said, holding arms out to her. "Bahar, I'm not pitying you."

She pointed at him. "You can't tell Jake any of this. Promise me you won't. Do you promise?"

He nodded.

She bowed her head. When she looked up, her face, in the dark light, was a mask of regret. "I used to be a better girl—I swear," she said.

"I know."

"If only you'd known me then, Drew. Before it was too late."

"No," he said. "It's not too late."

She turned away from him. He watched the long muscles of her legs shift as she left the room.

When the front door closed, he hopped up from the sofa, burst out of the little room, and went over to the dining-room window. He peeked out. He flicked off the overhead light. He stood there in a pale dark room, watching Bahar on the front porch.

She was stepping into clothes, shoes. She was illuminated by security poles lighting up one two three as she made her way down the long front path. The sky was plummy black. A light drizzle, a mist, fell sideways. Bahar walked past her car. She walked past a tree. Another security pole flared, giving her a long shadow. She walked past Jake's car. She walked across the street to the mill. She stopped. A pole flared. Her shadow bent around the side of the mill, up the grassy hill, and then she disappeared.

Lightning climbed the distant sky, and then there was dark.

Drew watched, fingertips to the window, waiting. A clock's cadence beat inside him.

After a minute, headlights flooded out from behind the mill, flicked to high beams. But no car zoomed into view. The blare of white light made every whiskery weed glow. It turned the gentle, unexpected rain silver.

"Whoa there, Bahar," he said into the window, and before he really knew what he was doing he was out the front door, pulling on a shirt, following her.

14

As Drew rounded the back corner of the mill, he saw noiseless white ducks gliding across the stream. They climbed the far banks, gathered beneath forked trees. Heat lightning flickered low purple and red.

The car was directly in front of him, engine humming quietly, headlights on, windows down, smoke wafting out the driver's side. It was a dark BMW 540i with brand-new Pirellis, and it was empty.

Drew came up beside it, put his head inside to double-check. A cigarette burned a tube of ash on the floor. He leaned down and picked it up, put it out in the ashtray. The filter was black and waxy. As he pulled himself out of the car, he looked up, looked a straight line out the passenger-side window, past the gray knotty branches hiding him from the stream, and saw them. They were down on the craggy bank, kneeling side by side.

"Well shit," Drew said. "Who's that?" He made his way

around the front of the car, pushed through the thicket, and came up behind them. Foam lapped at his feet as he splashed through the shallows.

Bahar looked over her shoulder at him, wincing. "Drew! Would you help me?" Black clouds washed the sky behind her.

He stood motionless, a body-length away from her. He could see the boy with her now. A tall, cadaverous, kneeling boy, his skin a watery blue in the moonlight. He wore black jeans soaked through, no shirt. Bahar held him as his long back heaved and he vomited into the water.

"Drew?" she cried again.

He lurched toward her. "Tell me what to do. I'll do anything. I'm here." He stood over them, watching how Bahar held the skinny, wretching boy. Her hands knew his body well, all the bones of his shoulders, the notch of his elbow, the cowlicky back of his ice-blond head.

"Give me your shirt," she said. "He's cold." Her hands trembled. "Here, give it to me."

Drew pulled the T-shirt over his head and put it in her hand. "What else do you need? What do you need me to do? Do you want me to call an ambulance? Do you want a doctor? What's wrong with him, Bahar? Tell me what to do."

The boy rose up from his hunched posture, shaking his head.

"No," Bahar said, draping the T-shirt over his shoulders and patting his wet back so the material clung to him. "No ambulance. No doctor. We'll be okay."

"Honey, what's the matter?" Drew asked.

"Honey, you okay?" Bahar asked. She wasn't talking to Drew. A light seemed to shine in her eyes when she looked down at the boy. She rested her face on his back as intimately as if he were a son. Her hands streamed down the back of his head, rubbing rain away.

"I need a down," the boy said. His voice was deep and formal, grief-stricken, almost British. "Baby, please. Take me back to the car? Can't you just take me back to the car?" He tried to straighten up his back. His spine rose through the wet T-shirt like a metal snake.

Bahar's brimming eyes met Drew's. "Help us," she whispered.

"Yeah," Drew nodded. He scooted to the boy's side, put his frail arm over his shoulder, and, on three, he and Bahar lifted the boy to his feet.

Her eyes met Drew's. Her chin trembled and she mouthed "Thank you."

As they carried him through the trees, the boy turned to look Drew right in the face with an unwavering, blinkless gaze.

"Are you okay?" Drew asked him.

The boy nodded soberly, murmuring softly, while Bahar talked over him, a string of "Here we go, here we go, here we go . . ."

He was so light it was like carrying a kite, with feet just barely lifted off the ground.

They put him in the backseat, and Bahar walked around

to the driver's side and looked across the top of the car at Drew. "Don't tell Jake," she whispered. "Not one word."

"This guy's a secret?" Drew asked.

"I'm asking you to take my side on this, Drew. Don't tell him anything about this."

"For now, I won't."

"Not one word."

"I won't," Drew said. "But *you* owe me the story—later."

She shook her head, hardly looking at him. "Later. Yeah."

"Who *is* he?" Drew asked. "How come I don't know him?"

"Later," she said.

Suddenly, the boy's head and shoulders pushed out the window. He looked blearily at Drew. "You *do* look just like her. Just fucking like her."

Drew watched him sadly for a moment before he saw the upside-down Polaroid in his hand. The boy flapped it at Drew, a flash of red on the picture-face, within the white border. "Look at this," the boy hissed. "You look just like her."

Drew held the face from the photo in his head for a moment. A girl. Sunburned. Smiling. But then he lost her; the face dissolved in his mind.

"I have more," the boy murmured, almost to himself.

Drew took a step to the car and held out his hand, and in the line of his vision he saw an open shoebox full of Polaroids on the seat beside the boy. "What's this?" he asked, leaning forward. His fingers grazed the photo and he opened his hand to take it. Would this shot look like the ones Bahar compulsively snapped?

"Don't!" Bahar shouted.

The photo slipped across Drew's palm as the boy withdrew inside the window, still smiling blankly. "I have more pictures," he lamented.

Bahar pulled her door open. She leaned into the car, pulling roughly at the boy's shoulder. "Shut up!" she ordered, and yanked him toward her, pulling him back inside.

"Bahar," the boy moaned. "If he was a girl, he'd look exactly. She could be his sister."

"Sshh," she said. "Sshh baby." She pried the Polaroid out of his hand and threw it, facedown, in the shoebox. But when Bahar tried to lift the box from the seat, the boy lurched up, making a dismal noise that rose from his chest. He hooked his fingers over the corner of the box and pulled it toward him.

"These are mine," he said haltingly.

"Of course they are," she said.

The boy turned his face to look at Drew through the wide-open window. "Tell her these are mine. For me to decide who sees them."

Just when it looked to Drew like the boy was going to lift up one of the Polaroids again, Bahar leaned over to the boy, whispering soft on his ear.

Slowly, his hand moved away from the box.

"That's okay, honey," she said, and her face was warm

now; it was a mother's face again. "That's okay. Lie down sweetheart." She looked through the window, looked up at Drew and gave him a gloomy smile. "Just let us take care of this, Drew."

He nodded.

Us. Just let *us*.

After she had the boy lying down, she buckled herself in. For a moment she just sat there, staring ahead with her door open like she might make a run for it. But then, abruptly, a shudder went up her back. She slammed her door shut, gunned the engine, and ripped down the grassy hill to the road.

Drew stood alone in the mill's night shadow and watched after her taillights. With a surge of what felt like seasickness, he had to sit down. He watched out into the dark, watched the fading reds and tried to swallow, rocking, holding his knees. It hurt him deep into the pit of his belly, this secret of hers. It hurt him like a solid gloved punch. He lay back in the grass and looked at the sky and wondered, really wondered, if the stars receded infinitely. At the moment, there was nothing he wouldn't believe.

15

The front door hung wide open and the foyer was tracked with wet footprints. The kitchen lights were off. An open beer, Jake's, sat on the counter. The can was still cold, dewy. Drew sucked down half of it in two long swallows. He fumbled in his pocket for the pills and swallowed one with another big gulp of beer. He breathed long, slow breaths, a hand on his bare stomach. Then he heard it.

A whirring noise came from the bar. A chattering noise.

"Hello?" he called.

The noise kept on.

Drew walked slowly down the dark hallway toward the bar, with his hands tensed at his side.

"Jake!" he called. "Hey, Jake!"

No answer.

The bar curved toward him. The whirring echoed on bare floor. It clicked like metal on metal.

Drew's eyes flicked from window to window. Outdoors, security lights flashed on and off, lighting up trees.

His breath hung in his ears.

"Jake?" he called, and then his voice trailed away.

He took a heavy step forward, and then another, and then the metallic noise blasted into thundering song. He flinched and then he laughed. *Fuck*, he sighed to himself, you freaking wuss.

It was just a skipping jammed-up CD on the stereo: Neil Young sang "Welfare Mothers" over a piggy electric guitar. The noise bounced off the walls.

Drew went out the back door, calling for Jake. He walked over to the pool and then around the perimeter. The line of woods, all lighted, gaped open before him. He watched into the deep dark. The memory of the white flash he had seen there earlier tickled along his shoulders, and he turned away to look across the lighted pool at the house.

Upstairs, every light was off. There were eight windows across the second floor, and six across the third, every curtain drawn.

On the ground floor, the only light came from the dining room chandelier. It made dim white bubbles on the window glass.

Agitation burned down Drew's legs. "Fuck it," he said, "I got no *time* for this." He started pacing back and forth the length of the pool, and as he settled into a stride he tried to see logic in what had just happened down by the stream. First, he asked himself, *what* did I see? There was the running car. The boy's blue skin and white hair, his bare bony back. There was Bahar, seeing him to the end of it, accustomed. A box of Polaroids on the backseat; one in the boy's spindly fingers. The cigarette burning in the car. No tracks on the boy's body. None of it made sense. The boy had driven over, taken the time to hide his car, waited for Bahar, and then decided to get high? Why was this guy a secret? Drew couldn't get it right in his head.

Then it was like a cold finger traced up his legs. A moment passed, just a moment, and Drew strained to listen closely.

Branches snapped behind him in the woods.

He turned his head slowly to look over his shoulder.

Trees settled into rows like teeth, a mouth of swaying leaves opening to a dark throat.

Drew hung there, twisted at the waist, watching the emptiness of the black woods, mesmerized.

It was as if the forest itself were reaching out for him. The branches and leaves were like arms and hands, and the wind was the whispering dead voice.

A shudder passed through the trees, and there was a high, flat animal cry that Drew could feel in his chest. He couldn't tear his eyes from the dark hollows.

Another branch cracked. This one was closer, just past a line of tall pines and elms. Drew stood in place. His hands trembled.

"Jake?" he called. "Hey, who's there?"

Silence.

Among the dark limbs, deep in the mouth of tingling leaves, a sliver of white appeared. Drew watched as it grew fuller, like the moon on fast time. He watched the white rind become a face deep in the woods.

And then he ran, heart pounding in his ears, around the pool, into the house, locking the door behind him. Huffing loud, he ran down the hall into the kitchen. He turned the corner to the stairway and slammed into Jake.

"Whoa!" Drew said, and fell against the wall.

"Hey, hey," Jake said. He was in his bathing suit, wet, chest hair curled darker, water pooling around his feet.

"Where were you?" Drew asked. "Where *were* you, man? Couldn't find you."

"No," Jake said. "Where were *you*?"

Drew looked again at Jake's feet. His toes were muddy; a leaf was stuck to his ankle. Though Drew had planned, despite his oath, to question Jake about Bahar's sickly friend, now he hesitated. It was just a passing feeling, he was sure, but he sensed something a little bit fucked-up in Jake's voice, its glad-to-see-ya hardiness. He watched Jake for a moment and said, "You tell me first."

"I was looking for you. You left. Bahar left. I went all over to find you guys."

"Oh," Drew said, listening hard. Had Jake started to sound more like himself? Did he sound real? "You didn't know where I was. Of course you didn't."

"Yeah," Jake said. "*Oh*. And where *were* you?"

"Yeah," Drew said. "You were just looking for me." He smiled.

Suddenly, he felt fine again. Seeing Jake was like popping a taut balloon; it brought the backyard chase to an embarrassing and quick end. He was just fine. He hadn't seen anything. There wasn't anyone hiding in the woods.

"I was outside," Drew said slowly. "I guess I should tell you about it."

Jake grinned, lion-like. "Hey, can it wait just a few? I want to piss."

"Um, yeah. It can wait."

"And I can just take a quick shower? Please baby?" He grinned again with the same ease.

"Okay," Drew said. "But hurry up."

"Yeah," Jake said. "I'll hurry." He stepped up to Drew, and he ducked his face, and he licked Drew's neck, the hollow.

Drew went upstairs to the room that he always slept in on his visits to Lancaster.

The ceiling was blue and the walls were the color of toast. A double bed sat in the center of the floor on a tattered, coarse rug. There were two small closets; an old rack stereo with shoddy, peeling speakers; an armless black love seat; and a matching couch.

He flopped onto the love seat and picked up the phone, called home.

His brother answered on the seventh ring.

"Ty, it's me," Drew said.

"Yo."

"Were you on the other line?"

"Nah."

Hearing his brother's voice break across the airwaves settled Drew's spirit. He felt warmth tick up his legs, and he smiled at his reflection in the window.

"Ty," he said, "I need your advice."

"Let me sit down for this."

"Why?"

"I do my best thinking sitting down."

Drew was quiet. He rehearsed what he wanted to say to his Ty. A summary would be good. Not too many details. He had to boil down his complaint, his suspicion—whatever it was.

What exactly was it?

"Okay, go ahead," Ty said. "Doctor's in."

"I don't have much time," Drew whispered. "Jake'll be back."

"So this is about Jake."

"No."

"Then what?"

"Ty, I'm feeling betrayed."

"Who by?"

"Bahar."

"Bahar," Ty mused, sounding sixteen. "What'd she do?"

Drew shifted in the love seat. "She kept something secret from me. And I can't make out the dimensions of the secret. Like, right now I don't know what it is. Not completely. But what I can't like be sure of is whether it's any of my business. Do you know what my stake is?"

"Are you going to tell me what you know?"

"I don't want to make it your business, too. You've got loads of your own commerce, bruh. You don't need more."

"Well, I appreciate that. I don't *exactly* know what to say. Is Bahar in trouble? Is it something you found out that you can maybe save her from? Or is this just a secret that hurt your feelings?"

"Hmmm," Drew said. "Let me think about that a minute."

"Take your time," Ty said, and started to hum "Kashmir."

Drew closed his eyes, listened to his brother imitate guitars and drums a thousand miles away. He thought it through, and one of the first things he concluded was that maybe Bahar just had a sick junky friend who she took care of. Maybe that was the whole story. Maybe it was a sign of her good character that she'd never spilled the boy's secret, not even to Drew. Maybe it just meant that, fuck, you could really trust her.

Ty stopped abruptly, murmuring, "Take your time."

Drew swallowed hard. His eyes burned a little bit. He rose up from the seat. "Ty," he gasped. "Brother, you're so right. Just my feelings hurt. I don't know the first fuckin' thing about it. Just my stupid hurt feelings. God am I glad I called you. Thanks, boy."

"Yeah, glad to," Ty said. "You're sure about it? Maybe it's a real thing. Maybe it's not just your hurt feelings? Are you sure?"

Drew took a deep breath. "Fucking *me*? I'm not sure of my damn name. But I'm definitely the king of hurt feelings and making book on them like they're always the other person's fault. So your like analysis comes as a welcome antidote. Totally. I'm going to take a chance that you're right."

"Oh," Ty said hesitantly. "That's nice, man."

"Yeah," Drew said.

"You can tell me more. I'll listen."

"Nah," Drew said. "I don't want to think about that anymore. I have my own secrets."

"From Bahar?"

"Probably. You know what? I'm gonna let you go. I don't wanna keep you."

"Are you sure? I won't make you talk against your will."

"Yup. I'm sure. Thanks, Ty. Hey, tell Mom I called."

"Goodnight, bruh. I will."

Drew hung up and walked to the door. He clicked it locked and unlocked, swinging it back and forth, listening for Jake's shower. He didn't hear anything in the house. He stood quietly for a while and listened. Still nothing.

He was about to go for a walk, find Jake in his room, when he noticed the envelope pinned to the plastic suit bag that hung on the inside of the door. For a moment, he just stared. His name was written on the envelope's face in block letters.

"Um, what is this?" he said out loud, and then he unpinned it from the suit bag, tore it open.

He read Jake's small handwriting on the plain card, a note to Drew with today's date at the top. "My suits hang a little big, so I took the liberty. Bahar said you liked this one when you went to New York. I took your inseam when you were asleep."

Drew unzipped the bag halfway and slid it off the suit jacket shoulders. He held it, the black wool Gucci, and he ran his finger up the crease in the pants on the hanger. Before he knew it, he was chuckling to himself and pulling off his bathing suit. He put the trousers on, and then the coat, and even though he wasn't wearing a belt or a shirt, he could tell that the suit fit just the way a suit was supposed to fit. It was almost tight without being tight at all. He stretched from side to side, and the suit stretched to conform. He walked across the room, just to see how it felt to go across a room in wool that had been cut and sewn into thousands of dollars.

Not a problem. It felt good.

It felt almost *too* good. Drew knuckled the wall with sluggish punches. He butted his forehead against the window. Man, he said to himself, what am I doing? Am I like a would-be player? An easy lay? Am I the guy who doesn't just sort of *jokingly* think he's enriched by a suit, a new black Gucci suit, but who actually like *experiences* that transformation as if he deserved it, as if it were a moral victory?

He shoved the window open and leaned out. He listened a while to the swaying whisper of the trees. Branches scratched the bricks and Drew reached out to grab the full green leaves. They were flat and speckled with dew. Their newness passed into Drew's pores like a virus. It was like his whole body absorbed their green blood. He breathed in deep sweet air, leaning further out into the night. He closed his eyes, wondering why he felt so good, all alone in a new black suit. He opened his eyes, and it was like the air itself, so full of secrets, was kissing him. The clean expensive air. He just closed his eyes. He just smiled.

There was a rap on the door.

"Come in," Drew called, pulling away from the window. He took a second to wipe his eyes, and then he turned around.

The door swung slowly open, and there was Jake, smiling, in a white-notched V-neck T-shirt and boxers. Black hair coiled up his chest. He smiled, pointed at Drew. "Yo cuz, you look sly. And that coming from me, a player-hater."

"Over here," Drew said. "Come and let me get some."

"I'm there," Jake said, but he held back, smiling.

"I don't deserve all the good stuff I get from you. I'm just dumbfounded, man. I don't deserve it."

"Ya don't have to do it alone," Jake broke in. "I don't even *want* you to make it alone. I want to be part of the strategy."

"A Gucci suit is not a scholarship is what I'm trying to say. I mean, fuck, no scholarship made me feel like this."

Jake looked at the floor for a moment, and then lifted up his face and gazed across the room at Drew. "You *love* me. I know it. I feel it. I know *you* love *me*, my imperfect asshole self, my boring suburban idiot self, and *I* love *you* for the way you are, for the way you look all dressed up in fancy clothes and the way you look when I take them off you, and I also love you for your aspirations and stuff and so many retarded things you say to hide your ambitions as if they're like shameful."

Drew, smiling hard, said, "That was really nice."

"Oh," Jake said shyly, "so now you're gonna make fun of me."

"But I'm not. I'm just inadequate to the task of matching so many great things you do for me, great things you say to me, that thing you have that makes you so strong."

Jake shrugged. "Yup. Trying."

"I don't know what the hell I mean. See, I have this one thing over here with Bahar. And we have the hardest two years of our like *lives*, like pre-med, in which, somehow, through some weird osmosis, we've gotten to know each other. And I'm not there yet with you, but I can tell you, standing right here right now, I see us having that, you know, in a matter of fucking *hours*. Like it is so close to us. All the time I spend with you makes me love you so much more. We're at the tipping-over point, where it's just going to overflow. I don't honestly know how much more room there's gonna be for anyone else—now that I'm having this with you. I'll close everyone else out of my life, I promise. I don't care about anyone else."

"I'm not gonna be satisfied until you feel like our history's more important than your history with my sister. I don't mean that in a hard way, but I do mean it."

"We're so close to that," Drew said. "Ya know, tonight, we're so close. I'm starting to feel like we're right on top of it."

"Well let's *get* there," Jake laughed, and he pushed the door shut. He came up against Drew and helped him out of the suit jacket. "Whatever works, let's do it."

Drew threw the jacket over the back of the love seat, watching Jake's eyes. "What's the matter, babe?"

Jake shook his head, looking past Drew.

"You seem like you're scared of something. Your eyes—where are you?"

"I'm right here," Jake said, nodding sharply.

Drew saw the fear shift across Jake's face, like there was a second face inside him that you could just barely see. "I see you there," Drew said. "Now tell me what's up."

"I don't want to talk anymore. That was hard for me. Just to talk like that right now. I can't talk anymore."

"Okay. I won't make you." Drew stepped out of his pants and laid them on top of the jacket. In one movement, he reached out to pull Jake by the waistband and fell back onto the love seat. Jake's boxers slid down as he landed sitting on Drew's thighs. It only took a second for Drew to push Jake's T-shirt up his back and open his mouth on the low knot of muscle right above the split of his ass.

Jake shuddered, pushing his ass up Drew's legs, pushing back against the top of Drew's head as Drew licked him.

"No," Drew murmured, "you don't take over right now. Let me."

"What?" Jake said slowly. "You want me just to be here?"

"You're just there. Yeah."

Jake's back relaxed against Drew's face, and Drew

pushed his tongue down into the light fur at Jake's crack. He let himself sink into the cushions, reclining, inching the boxers off Jake. Drew kissed his soap-clean skin, licked the hair on his legs until it was matted wet.

Jake pulled off his T-shirt and Drew reached around to hold his chest, pushing his fingers through the wiry hair. "Okay, want some?" Jake asked. He twisted his face around to look at Drew.

Drew pulled his tongue in, smiling. "Well yeah, man. Weren't you liking my technique."

Jake turned over on top of Drew, lay his mouth next to Drew's ear. "I was about to shoot off, fucker. Yes, I was liking it. Where do ya want it?"

Drew saw a dark light pierce through Jake's eyes again. "Hey my man, what?"

"Nothing," Jake said, licking the side of Drew's face.

"You're lying to me."

Jake was quiet for a moment before he pushed himself up, arms locked, and looked down into Drew's face. He slipped down Drew's body until he was sitting on his ankles and he bent his face down to take Drew's dick in his mouth.

Drew whimpered. It was the first time Jake had blown him; he'd forgotten how warm a mouth is. He looked down at the hard shoulders and the thick arms, the way Jake's muscles shifted as he held Drew with his tongue.

In just a couple of dozen licks and kisses, Drew was ready to come, so he pulled out of Jake's mouth and made himself remember a Cell Bio homework from spring semester. His chest huffed as he got up on his knees and kissed Jake's mouth hard.

Jake got him on his stomach. Jake kissed him all over, roughing his cheeks and chin up and down Drew's back, holding him down, fixed, to the bed, pushing his legs apart and then licking him.

"Okay, that's enough," Drew said. "You salty fuck."

Jake's dick was hard against Drew's leg. "You want?"

"Yeah, but don't use one. I totally trust you, man. We're now going to tip over."

"Really?"

"I just want us touching for real."

"You sure?"

Drew murmured.

"I want that, too. That's amazing. We both want that."

Drew closed his eyes. "We're here. We're right here and we're alive."

16

Drew woke up facedown with his mouth open, wet on the inside slice of Jake's thigh, his forearm wedged along the sweaty cleft of Jake's ass, and his chest stuck to Jake's belly. He said, "What in the hell time is it?"

Jake lay still, staring at the ceiling with his hands clasped behind his neck. "It's after midnight," he said softly.

Drew watched a vein on Jake's calf throb, and the sight of it in rhythm relaxed him. He lay there in silence for a long time. He liked the way Jake's leg felt. He liked the way it smelled. "You'd make a fortune if you marketed your scent," he said quietly. "How hard would that be?"

He waited for an answer. "Jake?"

Jake's stomach rose and fell at a quickening pace.

"You okay?" Drew asked. He pulled himself up, kneeling beside Jake on the bed.

For a stretched-out moment, Jake's face was placid, but

then, biting the inside of his cheek, he began to shake his head slowly, forlornly back and forth. "No, I'm not," he said. "No, I'm not okay, not at all." He stepped his legs over the side of the bed.

Drew touched his back. "What?"

"I'm gonna tell you," Jake blurted between deep breaths, bent over his knees, looking at the floor.

"What?" Drew began to knead the tense muscles in his back. He recognized that this gesture was powerful—holding someone when they were at a weak moment and you felt strong. It made him feel a different way. It made him a different man. He pressed his forearm into Jake's back because he knew that would help him.

"You don't want to touch me," Jake said.

Drew stopped, looked at his hands on Jake's broad shoulders.

"Let go of me, Drew."

"What are you saying? What are you thinking?"

"I'm trying to get up the steam to tell you."

Drew heard the keen ring in Jake's voice. He pulled his hands to himself. "Okay, tell me."

Jake turned to look at Drew over his shoulder. "I'm sorry not to be the person you want me to be."

Drew winced. His pulse raced, thready and erratic in his neck and wrist. He could feel it. "I'm starting to feel weird."

Jake rose up from bed. "You have to listen to me, Drew. *Look,* look at me. What I'm going to tell you will change the way you see me forever." He stepped into boxers. Drew looked down at his feet and spotted his own boxers. He slid them up his legs.

"It's really gonna be hard," Jake said.

"No, it won't," Drew promised. He kept his eyes on Jake. "You, you—don't worry about that. You can tell me. Anything. That's a thing I can promise. It doesn't matter how hard it is."

Jake pulled in a heavy breath and started: "It was January in 1993. My best friend, a guy named Troy Starr—"

"Troy Starr," Drew repeated, nodding. "I never heard you talk about a guy named Troy Starr." He looked down at his hands as, just for a moment, the incident by the stream—Bahar, the running BMW, the thin blue boy—scrolled across his skin. He lifted his eyes, met Jake's, and said, "Go ahead."

"You got to *listen* to me, Drew. I can't tell you again that I want to just tell this story right now without interruptions. Let me tell you my story. Will you let me do that?"

Drew nodded. *Troy Starr*. He had to remember the name.

Jake watched him for a while before he started talking again. "Troy Starr and me were good friends with a girl who didn't go to our high school. She was this fucking *crazy* girl named Allison. I mean *crazy*, always-trying-to-kill-herself crazy, stalking-guys-in-parking-lots crazy, writing poetry about how she's a Nazi, she'll sleep with Nazis, her dad's a Nazi, her mom's a bitch, every dude she fucks is a

Nazi, her heart is Nazi soap. And when she gets in the mood, she's like the meanest hardest bitch you ever met. Like of course her and Bahar become good friends. That was predictable as hell. They sort of matched. They sort of paired off. Rich-poor versions."

He stopped. He pulled a lamp shade off the lamp on the bureau beside him and began to destroy it. He turned the wire frame taut in his hands until it was a misshapen blur of tan fabric. A fiery vein rose on his neck, and he scowled at Drew. Drew wouldn't look away.

"She went to Columbus High School," Jake continued in a numb voice. "When you drive from Baltimore, and you cross the river to Lancaster County, that first town there is Columbus. It has got a *sick* reputation, and as far as I'm concerned, after the nasty hell I got in, it deserves an even sicker one. Like you can get cheap-as-shit highs there. You can buy anything at Columbus High."

Again, he stopped. It was like he wanted to give Drew an out, a chance to walk away. And though it was tempting, Drew felt like he was sewn to his seat. He waited urgently.

After a bit, Jake started up again. "There were these times, hours and days, when you could love Allison. She changed the like air in the room. She'd make you feel smarter, bigger, quicker, in just a couple of words. Sometimes you thought she could read your mind. But the good stuff never lasted long. It never lasted. Girl came back with sharper teeth. There was a window of opportunity."

Drew nodded, watching him.

"There was a short window when she was good, but then she'd turn on you so fast. She had no loyalty. Underneath it all, well, she was just poor white trash. There's no other way to say it. It sort of pains me."

For the first time in his life, Drew thought he could really hate Jake. "Please don't talk about someone like that. I hate the way you just said that."

Jake watched him closely.

"I mean that," Drew said. "My whole fucking family probably, you know, fits *your* definition of poor white trash. I closely, um, identify."

Jake looked at the floor and actually moaned through his bit lips. He shook his head back and forth before he nodded.

"Thank you," Drew said quietly.

Jake walked to the door, creaked it open, looked out into the hall. He watched for a long, quiet minute, and then he shut it. He came back to the bed, stood over Drew. "My mom *loved* Allison. Used to be like, 'You watch this girl; she's gonna be a star.' They had some kind of hardcore *sympathy*. You know how that is. It's people, doesn't matter what kind of people, nothing like that, people with the potential to be best friends. *That* drove Bahar nuts. Mom would call Allison on the phone just like to talk. You should have seen, Drew. Bahar turned that year. It was 1992, dude. Mark the calendar with a black marker. Bahar *froze* that year. I *died* that year. Damn—when *you* came into the picture, and Bahar came home from school talking about you all the time, I was like, Good, she found like a new best friend. Finally."

He knelt down next to the bed, put his hands on Drew's knees. "You know how my mom's on *Larry King* tomorrow night? You can talk now, Drew. I won't break your head."

"Yeah, I know that," Drew said carefully. A moment of Tamar's phone call played back in his mind: *Jake absolutely loves you.*

"Larry *King*. Larry *King*. Why do you think she's going to get the whole fucking hour? Saturday night's not prime-time, but this is just the beginning. I guarantee you."

Drew shook his head. Tamar's new book would've gotten her the five-minute slot at the end of the show.

"Mom has me calling in on *Larry King*. There's a lawsuit. The whole thing is going to be big news. It's going to blow up. I get to talk to Larry King. I get to tell my side of the story."

"What?" Drew whispered. "What happened with Allison? Tell me. Tell me."

"Larry King forced my hand, Drew. I wanted to tell you in my own time, my own way, after we were solid like diamonds. We never quite got there, did we Drew?"

Drew smiled weakly. "What if I said yes?"

"You'd be sweetly lying—" Jake stopped abruptly and stood up, looking at the closed door. "Who is that?"

Drew listened for a moment before he heard the footsteps, and then a man's booming voice, downstairs. "Bahar!" the voice called over and over.

"That's Arnie," Drew said. Relief filled the cold pit in his belly. He felt warmer. He wanted to get out of the room. Just for a few minutes. Just to collect his head.

Jake nodded. "She was supposed to keep him away, Drew. She's not even here. We're supposed to be alone—you and me, Drew. I'm supposed to tell you the whole story. Arnie can't be here." He had wild eyes.

"I should go down and tell him she's not here," Drew offered.

"Yeah, go down there and shut him up before I do it."

Drew said, "I'm coming right back. I'm ready to listen for as long as you need me to."

"Just go, please," Jake said. "Make him go away." He patted a jittery song on his thighs.

17

The kitchen was empty, but Drew could smell the sharp citrus of cologne mixed with sweat.

Drew called for him. "Arnie, where are you?"

It wasn't just that there was no answer; the air was charged, as if Arnie were hiding, waiting to leap out.

He looked around the kitchen in second-ticking slow motion.

The thing to do, Drew told himself, is to just go, just move, just walk. He leaned forward, pushing, made himself shove the air as if it had a skin he could break. He shouldered through, calling out in a low wavering voice, "Arnie, are you fucking here friend? Don't mess me up like this."

Still no answer.

He thudded through the kitchen, down the hall to the barroom. The glass flickered with outside spotlights. He stopped, stood in the center of the room as drops of white light speckled the floor.

Slowly, the windows began to glow. They held the white-blues of the security lights even between stuttering flashes.

Drew walked quietly to the first window, peered out. The rise of trees beyond the pool sparked with flashbulb lights, and every silver treetop looked snowcapped.

He pushed his face to the glass, engrossed. To see the other end of the pool, he stepped back from the window, to the right. A chaise lounge floated in the water. Circus-colored towels hung on chrome ladder-rails, flapping in the breeze.

Out of the corner of his eye, he saw a flutter in the woods. One by one, the spotlights began flashing to furious life. Trees flared white and then, just as quickly, turned black. Drew tried to follow the line of white light as it moved toward him, from a place deep in the woods, closer and closer, over the pool, light sparking the water.

He stepped back from the window until he was hidden in dark shadows against the wall. He pulled in a deep breath. He held it in his lungs, watching. He waited. Blood knotted his throat like rope. He tried to blow the dead air from his chest but not one faint puff escaped his dry mouth. His shoulder slid down the wall until he was on his knees, eyes crinkled almost shut, still waiting.

And then it came. A blurry rush, a jumble of white and blue that stopped with a thump on the window. A glowing figure, tight against the glass.

Drew's face, hidden in the dark, was level with the

ribcage—bleached blue like the rest of him. He slowly lifted his eyes up the boy's stomach, chest, neck.

Drew bit the inside of his cheek, hand on his neck pulse, and he watched the boy, floating above him, look inside the house.

The boy's mouth hung open. His tongue was blue in the shining whiteness. His close blond hair gleamed blue. Drew's shirt hung on the boy's knobby shoulders, framing his square flat chest.

Drew shouted when the boy rapped on the window with his bony knuckles. The boy opened his mouth wider, mimicking. His eyes locked on Drew's, and he massaged his neck with his hand.

A patch of his conversation with Ty flooded Drew's ears: *Is it just a secret that hurt your feelings? Maybe you can trust her. Maybe it's a sign of Bahar's goodness.*

Drew rose to his full height. The boy was still taller, with four, five inches on him. Drew froze, looking up at him.

The boy smiled. He nodded. He stepped back, turned away from the house, and broke into a run across the deck and up, up, up the slope of woods until he disappeared.

18

Arnie stood in the kitchen, picking lobster from a bright red bowl. He was dressed for trial. His wiry black hair was cut short, and heavy stubble covered his jaw.

"Hey," Drew said, blinking, pointing back to the barroom. "Did you see that?"

"No," Arnie muttered disinterestedly, and continued chewing a piggish mouthful of lobster. His lips glistened.

Drew watched him for a moment before he noticed sweat running down the side of Arnie's face, down his neck. His shirt was soaked through to the skin, so you could see the dark tips of his nipples. A trail led from his belly button into his pants.

"Arnie?" Drew said. "Are you okay? Where'd you go? Where were you? Didn't you hear me? I was calling for you. Didn't you see the guy outside at the window?"

Arnie looked over at him, nodded, swallowed lobster. "I ran up, actually. From the driveway. I was out there looking for Bahar and I got this weird feeling so I ran. Didn't see anybody."

"What kind of weird feeling?" Drew asked softly.

"It sounds pussy," Arnie said.

"Tell me."

"Well, it felt like someone was following me, really close."

"I'm sure there was. I just saw him, too. Right outside."

Arnie shut the refrigerator door and went to the table at the bay window carrying a bowl of raspberries and a spoon. "My God, it was just a sense-memory thing, atavistic fear." He shook his head, muttering, "Don't be a little boy. No one followed me."

"I'm telling you someone was. I *saw* him."

Arnie shook his head. "Well then call the police. I'm tired."

Drew thought about it for a moment. What would he tell a cop?

"Go ahead," Arnie said. "Call 911."

"Look," Drew said, "if you're gonna be a prick, I'll happily, quickly leave you alone. Man, I was in the middle of something. It isn't only you who has stuff going on in his life."

"I didn't intend to summon you little boy. Where's Bahar?"

The words just hung in the air between them.

"What do you mean?" Drew asked.

Arnie licked a single raspberry from the tip of his spoon and chewed it delicately. "Where's my girlfriend?"

"What do you mean?" Drew said.

Arnie pushed the bowl away and said, "Okay, where *is* Bahar?"

"Man, I don't know."

"Okay, let me ask it another way. Is Bahar upstairs or is she downstairs?"

"Neither."

"What are you talking about?" Arnie asked. His neck hardened. His legs tensed in his pants.

"You told her you weren't coming," Drew said flatly. "I heard the conversation."

"No I didn't."

"When you guys talked tonight?"

Arnie glared at him, a depth of blackness in his eyes.

Drew went on: "I mean, she was upset. After the argument."

"Oh," Arnie smiled coldly. "After she fought with me tonight? Wrong alibi."

"Yeah," Drew nodded. "When y'all fought tonight."

Arnie shook his head. "*We-all* didn't fight tonight. I haven't spoken to her since lunch."

Drew kept his mouth shut in his burning face. His stomach was burred with gooseflesh.

"I haven't talked to Bahar since lunch." Arnie knocked the raspberry bowl to the floor and it cracked into a dozen sparkling red shards. He lifted his face up to lock eyes with Drew. "What did it matter to her? Why did she lie to you about it? What did she gain? I mean, what did she gain?"

Drew pointed at his chest. "It might have been *my* mistake. It was during a fight between me and her—"

"Wrong," Arnie said. "No. Wrong alibi. She can mess with your head, friend, but don't take up for her with me. I told her today, at lunch, that I'd probably see her tonight. And I called you this evening, too. You passed that message on, right?"

Drew nodded. A cold rock lay on his heart. "She was upset. It was the baby, Arnie. The hormones. Being pregnant."

Arnie stopped to take a deep breath. He opened up his mouth to say something, but then he changed his mind.

"The baby could be yours. You don't wanna hate her like this, do you?" Drew said.

"I can't have a fucking baby, Drew," he barked. He whiffed in and out loudly through his nose. "She's really pregnant?"

"Yes," Drew whispered. "Yeah."

Arnie turned to look out the window. Drew's eyes followed. He watched water capping below the dam. A fine net of mist hung along the banks. Arnie put his hand flat on the glass. "Lost that chance ten years ago. Lost my chance to be a father."

Drew shook his head, watching Arnie's back. "I'm sorry," was all he could manage to say. The words hung pathetically in the air between them.

Arnie pulled his palm from the window and shifted in his seat, looked over at Drew. "I guess I've been had," he said quietly. "Sure feels like hell."

Drew lifted up his hands, let them flop down. He wanted to be the man who knew how to comfort a guy in need. He took a step, and Arnie watched him, smiling, and said, "I'll be fine. I almost died ten years ago. I can live through this. It's just a blip."

"Yeah," Drew said quickly. "This is gonna feel like nothing." He felt like he couldn't turn away. He felt like he couldn't blink. And all he wanted to do was hunt down Bahar and make her fix Arnie—for starters. Fucking with Drew's trust like this was one thing, but you didn't play games with a person's illness; that was enough to earn a sentence in hell.

Arnie looked down at the table. "But you can do me a favor."

After a moment, Drew said, "Anything, man. You tell me."

"Just for my pride, don't tell Bahar that I was here. It's an awful lot to ask you, but, hell, I'm asking you." Arnie got up. He was soaking wet. He took Drew's hand. "Can I count on you?"

Drew stepped toward him, nodding.

"I can count on you?" Arnie asked. "Please?"

Drew shook his hand firmly. "Yeah you can count on me. I mean that."

Jake's bedroom door was shut. No light shined in the crack at the floor.

A bulging manila envelope lay against the doorjamb. Written in heavy black marker were the words READ THIS.

Drew stood at the top of the stairs, looking down at the hard block letters, Jake's urgent handwriting. It looked so pathetic, a cache of moldy love letters, old photos—whatever was in that tan envelope, Drew didn't want to read it. He didn't have the heart in him, not tonight. There was nothing left tonight because there had been too much tonight. Secret after secret until he felt like some kind of joke was being played on him. All he wanted to do was fall into a coma. Alone. In the room he usually slept in.

There had been that moment before Arnie arrived when Drew'd have listened to anything, but right now he couldn't. He just knew that he couldn't listen tonight. Fuck them all.

He started along the hall without picking up the bundle. Each footstep landed on a creaking floorboard. He wasn't thinking where he was going.

He made it halfway to his room when he heard Jake's door open with a bang. He stopped but didn't turn around. He closed his eyes and waited.

"Are you going to make me beg you?" Jake asked.

"No."

"You're not? It feels like you want me to beg you. I will."

"What's in the envelope?" Drew asked. It was hard not to make his hands into fists. Tension lay like a rod down his lower back.

"Clippings. Newspaper clippings. The whole story."

Drew wouldn't turn around. "How bad is this story? I mean, it has to be bad. I understand that."

"Very bad."

"Can I read them in the room with you right there?"

"No."

"Can I read them in the morning?"

"No."

Drew kicked the wall. "Why can't you just tell me? How come I have this all coming down on me right now? You and me were on some kind of new-love ride, baby, and on my side it was a little scary, but I thought it was just the kind of scary that comes with strong feelings. But from your side it was something else, wasn't it?"

"No," Jake begged. "I *am* in love."

"But there *is* something else, isn't there?"

"If I didn't feel this way about you, I wouldn't be sharing a story like this."

"You're not *sharing* anything," Drew said. "It's so hard to be calm about this." He slumped against the wall and slowly turned so his face slid over the paint before he was looking right at Jake's gleaming eyes. "You were going to tell me. Before."

"I lost my nerve," Jake whispered.

"Well," Drew said, "when I look at your sad face, I know that I'll do anything you want me to do. I mean that."

"All I want you to do is know my past," Jake said, palms out. "But you have to want to. I mean, if you really don't want to know my whole story, you can leave right now. Take my car. Keys are out on the kitchen table. I'm serious. You can go."

"You've got me," Drew said. "You've got me. Regardless."

"Thank you," Jake said, and nodded curtly. He squatted to nab the envelope. He held it out to Drew. His eyes were large and flickering, and the light was going out of them. "No, it's more than that even. It's more than I have ever said out loud, but I have to show it to you. You have to see. I can't even just tell you." He turned away, crying. "Ah, it's true, Drew. Not everything they say in here, not each word—it's all so bad and so evil." He let his arm, the envelope, fall to his side. "This isn't what happened, but this is what I was accused of, and you can't understand me if you don't know, to start with, what people thought I did."

"I don't know," Drew hesitated. "Now I'm afraid."

Jake's voice fell to a whisper. "Let me be honest with you. I don't think you're going to come out of this a happier person. I'm asking you to do it anyway. I'm asking you, even though you feel it already, that it's not something shiny or good. It's more than you should have to do, but I'm asking you anyway. Fuck, I'm exploiting you. I'm abusing you. But even so, I do love you. Even if I never, never get to say it again."

"Why me?" Drew whispered. "Why is it so important to tell *me*? Me of all people? Maybe I should just leave. Jake, we've been like hooked up for six weeks. How come you have faith like that in me?"

"Because I can trust you," Jake said, wiping his eyes with an open hand. "You're enough like me that I can trust you.

And you're enough *better* than me that I can trust you. For me, Drew, it seems like you're the perfect person to confess to. I guess that's not a fucking compliment, is it? You're not perfect, but you're right in my sight. You came to me for a reason. That doesn't scare you, not really, does it? Because the way I think of you, you're not scared of bad news."

"I'm so totally scared of bad news."

"Are you scared now?"

Drew squinted at him, trying not to cry. "How should I know?"

"Do you trust me?"

Drew didn't answer.

"If you read this, it's the worst possible version, and it's wrong. I swear I swear I swear. I'm not as bad as this. They made it up, a lot of it. But I want you to know what they said about me when it first happened. That's the only way you'll understand me. I can tell you the truth after that. I will. I will."

"I don't care if I know or not. Don't show me. I'll trust you man."

"We're not *gonna* be the same," Jake said, "but I have to show you."

Finally, Drew said, "I know. Okay, I know."

"I can't make you, Drew." He held the envelope out. He turned to look at the wall. His whole body trembled.

Slowly, Drew reached out.

"Thank you," Jake said.

19

The girl's full name was Allison Kate Myers, and Jake killed her with a nine-inch hunting knife. He'd raped her first, anally, and he stabbed her eleven times.

But she lived, the police detectives said.

Jake's friend, Troy Starr, raped her next, as she lay dying, and then he gouged her throat open.

But she lived, the police detectives said.

Jake picked her up and carried her through her house to a pit in the backyard. He threw her in the pit. A slush trail of bloody footprints led from the fenced-in city lot up the steps, up to the back door, through the kitchen, into the living room. Jake sat for a while in the living room as Allison's skin died. The temperature that morning was eighteen degrees.

But she lived, the police detectives said.

There were marks in the snow, like she'd tried to write their names, but detectives surmised that when Troy saw her, from the kitchen window, moving, he went out back and stuck the knife all the way through the back of her head.

Jake carried her inside the house, threw her on the couch.

The boys drove to school, attended classes that day like they had no worries.

This was the story the newspaper reported. This was the story the police put together.

The story was constructed with forensic evidence, because Jake and Troy denied everything. The demeanor evidence was tough, since the boys were popular and no one would say a bad word against them—not a word.

This was the story according to the *Lancaster New Era*. It was in Article 5. It was in Article 98. The newspaper clippings were numbered in black marker. There were so many of them.

Drew had skipped ahead before he stuffed the articles in the manila envelope labeled READ THIS and dropped them to the floor.

He popped another Ativan. Twenty minutes before it would kick in.

He sat on the bed with the lights on and the door locked. The silence was awful.

Later, rapid footsteps approached his door, then stopped, and Drew jerked awake, lifted up from the pillows. His head was woozy. He blinked hard and swallowed.

Wake up.

Something kicked the door.

The muscles in Drew's back knotted up into his neck. He stayed perfectly still.

If he gets inside . . .

Drew jumped off the bed. "Fuck," he whispered. He looked over at the window, wondering if he could jump to the backyard. He sure could.

A loud rapping on the door.

If he has a knife . . .

The whole door rattled as someone pushed from the hallway. *Get your head together boy.*

Drew stood, rigid, forearms braced in front of him. He tried to breathe, but it was like his throat down into the cilia of his lungs had slicked over with cold.

The doorknob jiggled, didn't turn.

In spite of himself, he whimpered softly and watched as the door banged inward.

You've got to wake up now!

The door thudded again, shoulder-blocked.

It was possible that he would die, standing right here. He'd piss, and he'd shit his pants, and he'd drop dead on the spot.

Gutless.

He looked down at his hand.

Cowardice becomes you. It's your best feature.

Because that's what you are. That's all you are.

When he closed his eyes, a face rose up against the screen of his eyelids like cherries in a slot-machine window. It was blurry. And then the features sharpened into his brother's face, and there was something too foul, too deathly, too full of good-bye in seeing Ty, seeing Ty in his mind's eye when all he wanted was comfort. If you couldn't have comfort when you died, then what could you have?

He shook his head, fast, to fight off his drowsy buzz.

I'm not going to die. Not tonight.

"No fucking way," he said out loud. "Jake, I'm coming to the door right now. And you're going to talk to me. I'm not scared of you. I've already called people. People know I'm here. I'm coming to the door now. Jake, here I come. Cops. My brother. Bahar. There're a lot of people who know I'm here."

Silence. The door stood there, blank white.

"Jake!" he barked, and took the four steps to the door, took the knob in his hand, unlocked it, and pulled the door open with a whoosh of icy air.

The hallway in front of him was empty black. Before he had an idea to stop himself, he lunged out into it, looked right and left for Jake.

Nothing.

And as he looked down the hall to Jake's bedroom door with an oval of yellow light spilling out the crack at the floor, his back loosened up. He felt like he'd just faced down his doom. And maybe he'd almost acquitted himself.

Then a footstep creaked on the black stairwell.

The light under Jake's door vanished.

Darkness unfurled toward him like ink, and for a moment there was still light, a photo-flash of light burning in his eyes. Light that showed a face in profile, crouched at the top of the stairs.

The sound in the hall was a corpse's breath, a scuba-tank terror. *Hhhuh hhhuh hhhuh*.

He was alone with it.

He was suspended in the dark, unable to move.

With each hard second that ticked in his ear, the cold spread deeper up his legs, into his belly.

Another footstep clicked on wood. This one was closer.

And Drew wanted to meet it. He wanted it to hold him, smother him. He wanted to forget everything he'd learned and drown in this waking death.

Hhhuh hhhuh hhhuh.

It whispered to him.

It whispered his name.

Just the one word, his name, and the spell was broken.

"No!" he shouted.

He pulled back inside the room, shut and locked the door. His heart was round and tender in his throat, and he gasped for air as if he'd just surfaced from a weighted dive.

part two

20

Drew clicked his door open just a crack, and then, warily, he pulled it wider, until he could slip out into the hall.

He took one step. The floor squeaked.

It felt as if he were falling down the stairs, he was rushing them so smoothly, blood pumping in his ears. His palm on the polished banister slid beside him. He held the envelope filled with numbered clippings in his other hand.

The bowl Arnie had shattered lay in pieces on the floor. Drew stepped over it to grab Jake's Volvo keys off the kitchen table. A notecard was tented over them. Drew picked it up, read Jake's hand in black marker: I DON'T BLAME YOU FOR LEAVING.

With security lights flaring on and off, it was like he led a one-man battalion across a battlefield. But the lawn was so quiet, it was more like he had already died. His footsteps were the loud, steady percussion.

Then he saw it. There was a dark cop car pulled right up into the driveway, parked hard behind Jake's Volvo, blocking it in, and Drew's first feeling, a panicked irritation, gave way quickly to elation. He looked down at the envelope of newspaper clips in his hand and the first thing he thought was, It's over, it's all over. They've come for Jake. They've come to take him away. I can give it all up, and I don't have to do a thing.

He heard a soft sucking sound, faint behind him. The hairs on the back of his neck stood up.

He stood there, stock-still, and then slowly began to turn in a circle until he faced the quiet hungry noise.

He saw the back of the cop, standing on the side porch, in an ellipse of stuttering white light.

Drew opened his mouth to call out, but nothing came, no voice at all. He took a step closer and noticed the way the officer had himself positioned, leaning bent-kneed, a palm propped flat on the doorjamb. The cop had close-cut blond hair, broad shoulders, a wide neck.

"Sir?" Drew said.

The officer turned to look at Drew over his shoulder, and at the same time Drew saw the slender bare legs that wavered between the cop's dark legs.

Bahar, eyes red with tears, said, "Drew, this isn't really an excellent time."

For a moment it was like her face was a painter's trick,

like every line of the night's landscape led to her eyes in a dizzying, rushing blur.

"No, I don't think it is," he answered, and held up the thick envelope of clips.

"Yeah?" the cop said, with fury lurking in his voice. He gave Drew a long, thorough, contemptuous stare. "What's that you have? What's that you got in your hand?"

Bahar shook her head slowly back and forth and put her finger to her lips, as if to go, Sshh, Sshh. "Drew, this is Officer Lee Slaugh. We went to high school together."

"Bahar," Drew implored.

She kept watching him, shaking her head, staring Drew down.

The cop turned to look at her, and she dropped her hands next to her and resumed crying. "I don't *know* where he is, or where he's going," she said, "but I'm scared I let him down and I'm scared he's gonna hurt himself."

The cop said, "We've got to find him. Where do you think he's gone?"

"I haven't seen him all night," Bahar said. "When I talked to him, he was on his cell phone. I heard highway noise."

Drew watched her numbly, and he decided it was time to put an end to her act. "Jake's in the house," he said. "I saw him an hour ago."

The cop turned the whole way around, and now Drew saw how his uniform shirt was unbuttoned down to his belly, and his dewy chest pushed out, taut and suntanned, from the dark fabric.

Bahar held the cop's leg with her legs and looked at Drew. It was like she was happy that he'd turned Jake in. Her eyes sparkled and she smiled hard. "Oh," she said. "You thought I meant Jake."

Drew took a step backward, smiling sadly, shaking his head.

The cop disengaged from Bahar and started toward him. "We are *not* looking for Jake," he said. He buttoned up his shirt, moving in step with Drew, away from the house.

"We're talking about someone else," Bahar said. "Someone else entirely."

Bahar came up behind the police officer and put a hand on his back. A long moment passed as she whispered in his ear, and then she threw a glance Drew's way. "Did you have something else you wanted to go over with Officer Slaugh?"

Drew shook his head and let them pass him on the stone walk.

"I'll talk with you later," Bahar said, and she dipped inside the police car. She got settled in her seat before she stuck her head out and said, "We're going to find my friend."

The cop gave Drew a long stare before he got in beside her.

Suddenly, Bahar jumped out of the car, ran to Drew, and came up in front of him. "I wanted to tell you so many times. You'd never let me. But right now is *not* the time. I'm trying to save my brother's life here. You'll understand later."

"He killed that girl."

Again, she put her finger to her lip and went, "Sshh, sshh. Quiet, Drew."

And he realized that he was swaying on his feet. Her wavering face was all he could see. It comforted him, and he said, "You've, I mean you've got to stay with me. Or take me somewhere."

"Sshh," she said. "It's not the way you think it is, Drew. I promise you. Here, let me take you back to bed."

"No!" He shook away from her. "He's in there! I'm not going!"

"Baby," she whispered. "I have to go find my friend."

"Take me with you," he whispered.

"I can't," she whispered.

The siren lights fluttered against the swaying leaves and an intense short blast sounded. The cop car pulled out.

"Drew," she murmured, "I have to go. Here, lie down. Wait for me here."

He let her bring him to his knees. She petted his hair. "I'll be safe?"

"Drew, I'm coming back. You're safe. Just wait for me here."

He nodded, watching her back away from him. She turned to get in the cop car, waiting in the street. It hovered there for a long moment, headlights cutting the fog.

All of a sudden, Drew was alone.

When he woke up in the wet grass, Drew experienced Jake's low confession all over again.

You're like me.

You're not afraid of bad news.

Do you trust me?

The car door was unlocked. He threw the envelope on the passenger seat and pulled himself in. When he locked up, sitting quiet and looking out the windshield, the security lights fell dark. All the lights in the house were off except for the kitchen light. But he knew Jake wasn't sleeping. He was up there, watching.

Drew found the ignition key, pierced it into its slot, gave a hard turn, and set off the furnace blast of the car alarm.

Wipers scraped back and forth across the glass. The horn blew and the headlights pulsed on and off. The steering wheel clicked fast, stuck in place. A stern electronic voice proclaimed, "Step away! This car is protected!" He tried to open the door, but it wouldn't unlock. The electronic voice spoke louder. He pounded on the window.

In his panic to stop the noise, he reached into the back seat, fumbling for something heavy. His fingers went over the litter of Jake's building-site visits—wood planks, hinges, nail gun, carpenter's level, boxes of nails—until he found the heavy hammer. His hand closed over it.

The first thing he broke was his window. Glass didn't shower, not like in cartoon movies. He'd only chopped a hole. He spun the hammer in his palm and used the claw to chip away the veiny glass that remained. Then he stuck his head out to gasp in the pure air. He had that feeling in his stomach: too much food, too much drink, and the pills didn't help. He gagged and aimed for the grass.

* * *

His throat and nose burned even after he vomited. He spat out the remaining bile and pulled his head back inside the car. He had the hammer in hand, gripped tightly. The alarm shrieked on. Wipers scraped the dry glass.

He carefully put his hand on the door handle and pulled it. A weak click resounded from inside the door panel, but the lock just wouldn't give. The security lamps x-rayed the lawn.

He brought the hammer claw down onto the dashboard. The sound of plastic cracking soothed his eardrums, and he wanted to hear it again. He couldn't stop himself. Plastic and leather and thin wire fell under his blows. His vision narrowed until all that he saw in front of him were his fingers and the silver flash of the hammer's head. He beat the car. He quieted it.

21

To tell his mom or brother was out of the question, though he ached to call them, ached to unburden, ached to go home as if he'd never left New Orleans. But it would be like asking them to lick a line of poison powder from his lips so it didn't kill him. He just couldn't pull them into this night. If they were here, he wouldn't have anything to look for, to wait for, to long for.

What he needed to do, though, was talk to someone, now, right now, before he had a stroke.

He held the car phone tight in his hand, trying to remember a phone number. Who could he call? Who was there? Who'd be awake now—awake, at home, four in the morning on a Friday night?

Mary Hong would. Insomniac Mary Hong.

He punched in her number and waited, looking up through shattered glass at the big house looming over him.

Curtains hung solid like columns, pale in every window. He watched for ripples, for an odd angle.

On the sixth ring, Mary's machine picked up.

Drew hesitated for a moment, but when he started to leave his message his voice surprised him. It nearly failed him; it was like a tender old man's, asking for a nurse. "Mary," he said, "I know I shouldn't call you like this, but I need to see you right away. Is there any way I can see you tomorrow? I'll call soon as I get into Baltimore."

Right as he hung up, he remembered the slip of paper stuck in his back pocket. He pulled it out, unfolded it—a page of Duncan's Sylvia Plath book, a photo of the poet with Duncan's name and phone number written across her forehead. Drew hesitated for a moment before he went ahead and made the call.

Duncan answered on the second ring. "Hello?"

"It's Drew Burke."

"Ah, the annihilator," Duncan laughed. "What's wrong?"

"Can you talk?"

"What's the matter?" The smile was gone from Duncan's voice.

"Nothing. I just want to talk to someone." Suddenly, a shiver of tranquilizer went over his skull and he blinked twice, like he might be able to shake it away, but deep inside he knew better. He needed to brace himself: his beer and pill buzz was about to shout back into his blood.

"And I'll do," Duncan said, sucking on his cigarette.

"Should I spend time with you like this? The way you left things with me I didn't know we had anything to talk about. Am I wrong?"

After a moment, Drew said, "I don't know. You don't have to." He crinkled his eyes shut to keep from crying. "Just keep on doing what you were doing before I called. I just need the company. I'll owe you anything you want—okay?"

"Friend, what's the matter?"

"Please. Can't you just talk to me? Please?"

"Well, I can do that for ya, I guess." Duncan really did have a warm voice. "I was doing a jigsaw puzzle. Dorky, huh?"

Drew smiled into the phone. "Do they have dorks in Scotland?"

"Speak up, son. I can hardly hear you."

" 'M'okay, Duncan. Please just . . . stay . . ."

"Drew—you there?"

" 'M'here," he answered, and then his head rolled back and for just a moment he lost consciousness.

"Drew?"

"I'm back," he said. "Please don't let me fall asleep. You're here for me bubba, I won't forget that."

Duncan chuckled, and it sounded like music. Drew followed the laugh into the phone, walking clumsily through black space. When a light appeared, he shook his head briskly to wake himself up. This isn't working, he said to himself, and he used his thumbs to clasp his eyes open. He kept watching the light; it was a couple minutes before he understood that it was a flashlight shining in on him. A flashlight shining down from a window in the house. The light went back and forth across his shoulders and face. It pinned him to the seat. His eyes burned in the glare.

Yo, I should do something, he said to himself, but he didn't.

When he woke up, just a little bit later, his bummer curse of a buzz had burned off. He mumbled into the phone, "Sorry, I'm back."

"From the dead, huh?" Duncan said.

It was good to hear this guy lightly breathing in some other place—alive with a cigarette, a cup of coffee, doing a jigsaw at the end of a long workday. For a long stretch they didn't talk to one another. Duncan kept a running commentary on his puzzle skill, but he never asked Drew a question, never wanted to know why Drew had called at this hour, why he needed Duncan of all people to be there for him, why he couldn't stop crying, softer and softer like he was pacing himself, like he'd be crying until he died.

Close to an hour passed before he hung up with Duncan. There was a clear, calmer lens in front of his eyes now. He sat looking up at the house and thought through his options. For a moment, he saw them outlined crisply before him in all their dead wrongness.

He could just walk. But he'd left his cash, plastic, calling card, and ID upstairs, in his room.

He could sneak back into the house, gather his stuff, call a cab, and then wait for it up on the main street, Marietta

Avenue, a half mile away. But even *considering* that option made his heart drop into the black pit of his stomach. How could he walk back in that house? Alone?

He could try to get this car started. He looked at the dash, splintered and gouged, and smiled darkly to himself. *Yeah*, maybe I'll do *that*.

There was one thing he could do now, he decided, if he just made himself. Instead of just sitting here, afraid and weak.

He could take an appraising look through the newspaper, all the clippings, one by one until he really learned it—the whole savage story.

He could try to understand it. He could try to clarify, for himself, what Jake had confessed to, how much.

He could match the Jake he knew with the Jake who'd murdered a girl, who'd raped a girl, who'd tortured and maimed. There were two Jake Richards, and Drew had to make them one before he could rest. It was his obligation.

The pure silence was too pure, like sleep, and he had to get some noise, even buzzing static if he could find it. He snagged pliers from the toolbox on the backseat and turned the snapped, dead radio knob. Without noise, his high might sneak back on him.

Music flew crisply from the speakers: an old Keith Sweat hit, lover music, a sad, urgent voice cooing, "Maybe baby I know/maybe I love you so . . ."

Drew listened intently as he peeled open the manila envelope with his thumb. He toe-tapped as if working an air pump that would fill him with courage. The paper tore, and he looked inside. There they were: folded, paper-clipped, stapled newspaper articles. With a sigh, he turned the envelope upside down in his lap.

He found Article 1. His heart thudded in his ears as he began to read:

LANCASTER NEW ERA

January 12, 1993

COLUMBUS GIRL SLAIN IN HOME

Police Follow Multiple Leads

---

by Martin L. Shenk

New Era Staff Writer

A sixteen-year-old Columbus girl was attacked and killed in her home early this morning after her mother left for work at Susquehanna Valley Glassware and Linens. Police arrived at the grisly crime scene just before ten A.M., in response to a neighbor's 911 call. The victim, whose name is being withheld until family members are notified, was stabbed a dozen times and left for dead in the living room . . .

Drew dropped the article and looked in the sideview mirror. He thought he'd seen something out of the corner of his eye, the blur of white.

A current lingered in his legs.

He watched in the silver mirror for a face in the tree limbs, but there was so much to look at, a wide-screen vista. He couldn't make himself actually turn around in his seat to watch. What would he do if he saw someone?

He shook his head at his own weakness and picked up the next article, Article 2. It was five columns of print across the front with a big photograph of Allison Myers looking straight-on at the camera. There was a shimmering electric charge in her eyes. For a long moment, he couldn't look away from her face. He saw something familiar there, but it didn't come to him. Finally, he looked away from her.

He held the article flat under the unbroken domelight in the roof:

LANCASTER NEW ERA

January 13, 1993

NO ARRESTS IN COLUMBUS MURDER

Police Continue Investigation

---

by Martin L. Shenk

New Era Staff Writer

Columbus police continue to follow multiple leads in the ongoing investigation of Friday's brutal stabbing murder of a sixteen-year-old Columbus High School student, Allison Kate Myers. Classes were canceled today at the victim's school. Police investigated several leads amid rumors spreading like wildfire through this tightly-knit riverside community. New developments today include . . .

Drew's chin trembled. He turned himself in his seat to get as much leverage as he could and gave the door a hard kangaroo kick. He kicked again. The alarm whimpered briefly before drooping off.

He picked up Article 3 and Article 4 and held them beside one another, looking back and forth at the nearly matching headlines:

LANCASTER NEW ERA

January 19, 1993

KNIFE, BLOODY CLOTHING FOUND

Stream Probed as Investigators Focus on Hempfield Boys

LANCASTER NEW ERA

January 20, 1993

KNIFE, BLOODY CLOTHING ID'D

"Prominent Families," Investigators Say, Closing In

Drew didn't know what exactly made him wait so intently. What kept him from it? What made him deny the close look at the shot of Jake? Hours ago, when he first saw it, the photo had burned itself into his memory file, but all this time he'd been wanting to study it closer. Now, he held it in the light.

Jake was forty pounds skinnier, easy. He wore baggy jeans and a Hole T-shirt over thermal long johns and black shitkickers. A cop held him lightly by the arm, as if escorting him to a dance. There was a flash in the cop-car windshield. There was a flash up in the corner of the photo, in the dark photo sky.

Jake had the look of someone who'd been teargassed.

The way I kept you in my head, the way I saw you all this time. The way I kissed you and defended you. The way you filled up my fucking head and I would've given up anything, given up anyone, just to be with you, just to be you, just to be your shadow. And this—this is who you were.

He moved on to Article 5:

LANCASTER NEW ERA

January 29, 1993

WHO ARE THE HEMPFIELD "GOOD KIDS" CHARGED WITH BRUTAL STABBING?

Victim Dated Wealthy Sons of Doctors, Entrepreneurs

by Tina Crothers

New Era Staff Writer

Jacob I. Richards and Troy N. Starr were charged with stabbing to death sixteen-year-old Allison Myers, a sophomore at Columbus High School, but friends and teachers who knew the two Hempfield High School sophomores say they don't believe the boys are guilty. In exhaustive interviews with *New Era* reporters, students at Hempfield portray two gentle friends best known for their generosity and good looks. Richards, 15, the son of famed local psychotherapist Tamar Richards, and Starr, 16, the son of Lancaster Anesthesiologists founding physician Deirdre Starr, were active in the Lancaster Youth Alliance, which brought together students from the county's richest and poorest school districts for social activities and community service. Allison Myers was also a member of—

Drew stopped reading. He dropped the article on the passenger seat. He used the pliers to turn off the radio and sat in silence. There was a wind that bore through the trees, over the car, wildly whistling against the shattered windows.

This is how it feels to condemn, he said to himself. This big death where everything matches.

This is how it feels, then. This is how it feels to sit there in judgment, to sentence a man.

Jake, I sentence you.

As Drew lay back against the soft leather seat, his inner eye saw the dank, cool pit of Lafitte's Blacksmith Shop, a dilapidated neighborhood bar, flame-lit, deep in the French Quarter, back home in New Orleans. He could hear the tinny piano, the wasted laughter from the patio, the noise of rain pinging the windows.

His eyes were open, but for close to an hour he didn't watch, didn't notice, didn't pay attention. He was depleted, sedated, and hungover from steady beer-drinking, from Buspar and Ativan, from sex, from reading, from crying, from wishing the truth away. There was nothing he wouldn't give up to make the truth just disappear.

But then, all of a sudden, he held two photos in his line of sight. They lay on the passenger seat, amid the jumble of papers. One photo was part of a numbered newspaper clip; the other was on the torn book page where Duncan had written his phone number.

Drew's eyes drifted from one photo to the other for a minute before he made the connection between them, before he saw it, the blunt resemblance. A chemical taste flooded his mouth. He brought them up to the domelight, side-by-side. He could hardly breathe.

Drew ran his thumb across the faces of Allison Myers and Sylvia Plath until they blurred together. He brought them closer. He brought them flat against the light so his fingers glowed red through the thin paper.

They were doubles, if you wanted to see them that way.

Drew watched them. He wanted to see them that way.

They had the same lips, the same crinkly smile, the same dark eyebrows, and the same dark eyes. They had the same putty nose, the exact same round cheeks. They had the same ears. They had the same chins.

Sylvia had died more than thirty years before Allison, but it didn't matter. In these photos, the girls were blood sisters. They were mother and daughter. Allison was fatal Sylvia reincarnated, a bleakly smiling burning girl.

22

Drew lurched up in his seat, lightning-struck by one obvious, vital fact that he'd been ignoring: Jake wasn't in jail.

It hadn't occurred to him—not with any real force—while he was in the house, cowering. It hadn't occurred to him when he saw Bahar with the cop, either. Fuck, he'd been wanting to give mister police his bag of newspaper clips, like the cop couldn't read them down at the local library. He had nothing but public records in his hand.

This whole town knew what Jake had done. Yet he lived here as if nothing had ever gone wrong with his life.

That's why Jake wouldn't talk to me right away. It's just his test. It's just him trying to find out if I trust him. Because why should he trust me first?

How clearly he saw it now. Jake wanted something from him. He needed something. But what?

This town. This whole town trusted Jake. He went to

the local college, worked with the local builders and developers.

How come no one held a grudge?

There's got to be an answer in these clips, Drew thought. For fuck's sake, he wants me to trust him the same way this whole town does. He wants me to trust him more.

He thumbed the articles until he got to Article 41.

The explanation was right there.

LANCASTER NEW ERA

February 28, 1993

"WE DIDN'T KILL ALLISON MYERS!"

Richards, Starr Allege Evidence Tampering

---

by Martin L. Shenk

New Era Staff Writer

Attorneys for accused killers Jacob Richards and Troy Starr blew open the county courthouse with shocking accusations of police misconduct and prosecutorial tampering. During preliminary hearings yesterday, Richards's lead attorney, Rina Corvale, played an audio tape in which an officer seems to admit that a crucial piece of evidence, the hunting knife allegedly used by Richards and Starr to kill Allison Myers, disappeared from police custody for twelve hours the day of the murder. In related news, con-

> troversial police detective Chuck Weber was placed on administrative leave pending the investigation into the defense allegations. Weber's lawyer—

Drew placed the article carefully in his lap. His tears ran a couple of hot, stinging paths down his cheeks. His nose leaked. He punched the steering wheel over and over, until he had it straight in his head.

Poor Jake. Wrongly accused. A good guy after all.

There was proof, he told himself. Bad cops had framed Jake. A knife had disappeared from custody. Blood was planted. Hair fibers were mixed up. All the DA had was circumstantial evidence, messy circumstantial evidence. You could never trust it. You could never convict someone on it. Not once you had proof that the cops fucked with it.

Hell, that was as good as a free pass from jail.

Do I believe?

Drew picked up the article. He read on.

After a while, his stomach started acting up again, like there was nothing to celebrate.

Do I believe?

It was the alibi that made him feel this way. He couldn't get his brain to believe it. He kept reading it, over and over. But no matter how hard he tried, he couldn't forget how Jake had stood there in the hallway, just hours ago, and said, Drew, man, it's true, some part is true.

Isn't that how he'd said it?

Hadn't he almost confessed?

Jake was the killer, or he was the killer's helper, or maybe, maybe he was just part of the alibi, or maybe he's just, you know, the killer's fucking friend. Maybe that was enough to hate himself for, enough to feel guilty for.

Surely, Drew thought, I hate him right now.

Do I believe?

Hadn't he almost confessed?

Hadn't he?

But that conversation was gone now. It was already lost.

What strong powers of concentration you have.

And then, with self-doubt, came a little embryonic hope. Like maybe Drew had it all wrong. Maybe he'd misunderstood. Maybe there had been no attempted confession at all.

What do I believe?

Am I fucking strong enough to believe anything?

He went back to the text, the source, the essence. He read it again—the clip that laid out Jake's innocence.

The alibi was so simple. Jake and Troy were at Jake's, eating breakfast with Jake's mom, while Allison was being murdered. Tamar testified that Jake and Troy helped her clean up the dishes.

End of story.

God, Drew told himself, nodding. God, that sounds convincing.

God is that bullshit.

He flipped to the next page of the article.

There was a timetable that lined up the police version of the murder next to Jake's alibi. Every fifteen minutes was graphed out as if each side owned some kind of video documentation. Drew read it with mounting dread. How could they be so sure of the evidence?

6:45 A.M., 7:00 A.M., 7:15 A.M., 7:30 A.M., 7:45 A.M.—the two versions of what happened that morning played in his head like overlapping movies.

He thumbed the clippings straight through to Article 98:

LANCASTER NEW ERA

May 2, 1993

HEMPFIELD TEENS FREED

Judge Alleges Perjury, Misconduct; Bars Retrial

---

by Martin L. Shenk
New Era Staff Writer

Jacob Richards and Troy Starr walked jubilantly from county court today, free young men. Their attorneys' high-stakes gamble, forcing an exceptionally speedy trial, paid off in spades. During cross-examination of only the second witness for the prosecution, Rina Corvale forced controversial police detective Chuck Weber, formerly of the Columbus Police, to admit that he'd smeared the blood of Allison Myers on the 9-inch knife in his custody. Weber also admitted that he shook blood from Richards's and Starr's sample vials on the knife.

Following Weber's testimony, Judge John E. Darbell,

Lancaster County Court, immediately halted testimony. After a fifteen minute chambers conference with prosecutors and defense team, Darbell came back into the courtroom and told the two young defendants: "You are released from all obligation to this court and you shall not be retried."

Corvale's dramatic presentation of crime-scene photo enlargements brought gasps to the standing-room crowd. Using state-of-the art digital technology, Corvale's photographic experts re-created photos from negatives that she claimed had been deliberately damaged by Weber. The photos show the detective holding the knife at the crime scene and then again at the police station, five hours later, during a time when Police Chief Ron Kirchner held a press conference to address media leaks alleging the knife had disappeared.

When confronted with the surprise photos, Weber broke down on the stand and admitted planting blood on the knife because he was worried that snow, rain, and muddy water might have washed it clean.

The knife was identical to one that Troy Starr had purchased just ten days before the murder.

Other evidence, including the victim's blood on Richards's and Starr's clothing, were considered by many legal experts to be equally damning, but Judge Darbell left no doubt that he considered the evidence of police and prosecutorial tampering in the case the worst he'd seen in a thirty-five-year career on the bench.

Darbell's dramatic decision was met by raucous cheers

> in the courtroom packed with friends of the popular Hempfield teens. The family of the victim left the courtroom during Darbell's announcement. They remain in seclusion.

Drew was barely awake, just moving through the clips, one by one, looking at the photos and headlines and lead paragraphs.

He was finding it hard to pull Jake from Allison's house.

He was finding it hard to launder Allison's blood from Jake's T-shirt.

He was finding it hard to take the knife out of Jake's bloody hand.

He got to the end of the clips, skimming, and he lingered on the last one, Article 137. It had been published just two weeks ago, to lay out the ground rules for the civil case that Allison's mother had filed against Jake's and Troy's families, a ten-million-dollar wrongful death suit scheduled to start in June.

This article, point by point, convicted Jake and Troy with an avalanche of circumstantial evidence. The same reporter, in a side article, convicted the police of fucking with the evidence to make sure there was a guilty verdict. It made you accept the double whammy: Bad cops framed guilty killers. It was a sweeping overview of the case, everything you had to know if you wanted to put a hard verdict down on Jake's and Troy's heads in the June trial.

June, Drew said to himself. June. Weeks away, and I only just found out.

Why is he finally telling me now? What's been going on behind the scenes?

What does he want from me?

The photos and the newsprint blurred in front of his eyes, as if rain were washing away the ink. He was so tired that when a big photo, a shot he'd missed, shuffled to the top of his pile, it was all he could do not to yawn.

But the face took his breath away.

Troy Starr. A giant color photo of Troy Starr, part of a long news clip.

So this was Troy Starr, he said, sinking lower in his seat. A moment passed slowly as he pulled the article closer and closer to his face.

In the photo, Troy Starr stood with his parents on the courthouse sidewalk, smiling. He was tall, gaunt, blond.

That face. There was no way to mistake it.

Troy Starr was Bahar's friend from the stream, the blue boy.

Troy Starr, the accomplice.

Drew looked out his jagged windshield, out into the woods. It had gotten very cold outside.

Troy Starr. The missing friend Bahar was looking for with her friendly cop.

That boy wasn't missing.

He was here tonight. Close. Right now.

That boy wasn't missing, and Bahar knew it. Why was she taking an overgrown junior cop for a ride? Why was she wailing like her Troy was in danger somewhere?

That boy couldn't spit without her knowing.

Bahar and the young husky cop were not gonna find Troy Starr.

Because he hadn't gone anywhere.

He was here. He was somewhere in the trees.

Drew could feel it.

part three

23

Drew peeled his sticky, flushed face from the sweaty seat. He opened his eyes, slowly, against the bright light. His legs tensed outward onto the gravel driveway; sun fell on his bare ankles. For a moment he rested, undisturbed, but then, with a start, he saw it—the tan blanket across his lap. And the car door was unlocked, opened. When he sat up, a pillow slipped out from behind his head, falling into the space between his seat and the passenger seat. He grabbed it, held it to his face. The scent on the green pillowcase was the scent of Jake.

Jake had tucked him in.

Drew lifted out of the car, crunching glass with his sneakers as he walked a few wobbly steps, looking wildly around the lawn. A bee landed in his hair and then sped off. He leaned against the car, still shaking the insect away, and then he looked up and his line of vision pushed away the branches that hung between him and the house, shook the leaves, cleared a path for his bleary eyes.

Now he had a direct view of Jake.

Jake stood at the door, holding a Coke. He got larger even as Drew watched him. His features grew crisper. It was like getting a perfect zoom on your camera lens.

Drew took a step back.

Jake's posture softened. He almost smiled. He wore boxers and a white T-shirt. "Are you afraid of me?" he asked. He frowned and looked at the ground.

Drew regarded him for a long, hard time. It surprised him that he could still see the Jake he loved, but he could. His Jake stood right there. His Jake lived in the same body as the Jake who might have killed a girl, a friend. "Yes," Drew said, "I am."

Jake winced, but turned his eyes up at Drew. In a soft, rough voice he asked, "Do you hate me?"

"Yes," Drew said. "Right now I do. Right this very moment."

Jake's chin trembled. "Do you think I killed Allison Myers?"

Drew nodded.

Jake took a couple of steps toward him, palms turned up. "You stayed, though. That means something."

"No, stay where you are," Drew said, shaking his head slowly, evenly, back and forth. "No, I can't have you . . . come . . . over here. I can't."

Jake took another step, exaggeratedly slow. "I really want to explain."

Drew stepped back. "Jake, please. I *am* scared, man."

Jake turned his head to the side. "I understand."

It looked to Drew like he was almost smiling.

"That girl's still dead," Drew shouted. "*She* understands. You don't count!"

Jake stiffened. "I understand."

"The cops fucked up and you got off, but that's all I believe right now. All I believe is that you got off and I'm standing here talking to you and I'm wondering if you killed her."

"Drew—"

"No, you shut up. Last night I begged you to tell me, face-to-face. You had your chance." Drew came around the side of the beat-up car. Window glass crunched under his shoes. "That girl is still dead," he said. "I can't make that go away."

"Allison was one of my best friends. I know she's dead like a bullet in my face."

"I don't know you."

Jake's eyebrows knitted together and he dipped his face into the air like it was a pool. Then he looked up at Drew with his big, melting, brown floral eyes and said, "Let me explain."

Drew wanted to smile. He wanted this to be the moment when he reconciled with Jake. He wanted there to be a clear feeling in the air between them. He wanted to say, I understand, I'm here, let me be the one.

But he couldn't. Not when he *knew*, in his gut, that Jake was the killer.

He couldn't.

He wouldn't.

Jake whispered, "Let me explain."

Drew shook his head, quietly, looking at the ground. A pair of angry bees flew past his face. When he looked up at Jake, he saw a killer with a bloody smile, scratch marks up his arms. He saw a girl screaming, pulling on Jake's arms, shouting, Save me, help me, save me. Then he suddenly realized that the T-shirt he was wearing, a navy blue baggy one with the Coke logo in red script across the chest, was Jake's. He pulled the T-shirt away from his body, looking down at it with the nausea of mourning. With one swift motion, he pulled it off and threw it on the Volvo hood. He waited with his hands together behind his neck, glowering at Jake, and then a tiny quivering bee, just a baby, landed in the hair under his arm. Another fell on his elbow. Without thinking, Drew plucked them both from his skin, and with one in each hand he threw them into the air by their wings. A moment passed where they hung in midair, like toys on string, and then their wings buzzed loudly and they blew away.

"What if I did what I did for Bahar?" Jake whispered.

A hole opened up in Drew's brain. "What did you just say?" He had to fight to keep his balance.

"You heard me."

What if I did what I did . . .

It was a confession. He *had* killed Allison.

For Bahar.

For Bahar.

Got to stay calm. Got to get away. Don't panic. Don't let him near. Don't let him touch you.

He started to back away from the house, step by slow step. As he passed the car, he told Jake, "Don't follow me."

"Where you going?"

"Don't ask me questions."

Something dark crossed Jake's face. "What have I got to do? I got to tell you."

"I need to be alone," Drew said carefully.

Jake glided toward him now, quickly, like he was on wheels. A light flared inside Drew. His hands took Jake's shoulders, brought Jake toward him and then down hard, Jake's face on his forearm and Drew's knee up into his stomach. Jake sprawled back to the ground.

Drew's vision flickered. The house faded. The trees faded. No wind blew, and sweat rose up on his back. He wiped his brow with a damp forearm.

"Baby," Jake said, trying to get up on his knees, "don't leave me. Not for her."

Drew turned away from him. He picked up speed. He ran.

He raced up Redder's Road, each stride pounding heavy through his legs, but as he approached Marietta Avenue, where he had it in the back of his head to hitch a ride, his body slowed, throttled a moment, and stopped. The air coagulated around him, held onto him. It acquired a shimmering fullness. As he stood there at the empty intersection and looked out at the rippling grasslands, the rings of flooded green darkening toward the vanishing point, he began to understand just what a coward he was.

Here was an event, an actual event, that his weak spirit had reason to be afraid of. This wasn't just floating, empty neurosis, his dildo companion. Fucking no way. This was real marrow. Here it was—a moment that would maybe change his pitiful life, once and for all.

His own private heart of darkness and he was running.

It's true, he said to himself. Cold calm flooded his chest.

Now he knew. Now it was clear to him why Jake had insisted he read a sheath of newspaper clippings, cold documentation.

There was a reason Jake couldn't come right out and say it.

Jake was guilty. Drew knew it. He'd known from the first clip he read. He'd known from the very first headline. He couldn't talk himself out of it any longer.

But there was something more. There was a reason Jake gave up every article, even the ones that convinced Drew he was the bloody killer, even the investigative rebuttals to Jake's lucky verdict.

Jake *wanted* him to know. Jake *wanted* to tell him. Jake *wanted* him to believe.

And there was a reason Jake wanted to implicate Bahar, to say she bore responsibility, too. It was fear. Fear that Drew wouldn't be strong enough to help him. Fear that the only way Drew would do the hard thing was if Bahar were part of the equation, part of the murder.

For some reason, Jake needed *him*. God, did Jake need him bad, the way no one had ever needed him. And Bahar, she needed him too.

They were just the kind of people who *would* need him: selfish as him, mean as him, weak as him.

His people. His bad people.

When he said the words over and over in his head, it gave him a charge. He had always known these were his bad people, yet he had pursued them and staked out their loyalty. When it had been lively rich good times, he'd had no problem convincing himself that these were his best friends, but now he had an out. Now, if he wanted to walk away, he could just walk away. He could leave them behind.

But was that what he was supposed to do? Was that the kind of friend he was?

Maybe now it was his time to be devoted in return, to be devoted no matter what. Friend for life. Wasn't he strong enough to be a friend for life?

There wasn't one important person in the history of the world who hadn't stood by a bad husband, friend, or mother. You saw them everywhere. They glowed with dark allegiance. It was the hard cold truth.

If he left now, he might as well just keep running back home, to New Orleans, back home and never leave.

He shook his head slowly and looked at the sky.

The sun came down in spotlights through blackening clouds and caught the underside of bending trees.

Jake. He cut that girl up.

Just hearing the word, just hearing his name, Jake Jake Jake—it sounded so different in his head, so ugly, like the secret translation of some deadly curse.

If I'm afraid, he said to himself, does that mean I've got to run? If I'm afraid, couldn't I still find—somewhere in me—an ounce of physical courage?

Don't I have one ounce?

Before he could think himself weaker, he turned around and in a couple of minutes made the curve of Redder's Road. He kept going down the rock path behind the mill into the icy clear green stream where the dam spilled over. He leaned forward into the rough water to soak his head. A cap of cold shrunk on his scalp. He shook, and needles of water flew off. He dug his sneakers into the rocky bed and soon his feet were icy. But he stayed and walked close to the falls. Tumbling spray broke across his shoulders and chest, and for a long minute he stood there, soaked, gritting his teeth. He tried to keep his eyes open in the sheer face of the water.

Here's my fucking reservoir, he said to himself. He looked at his hands and slapped them together for the noise of it. He gave a loud shout as he pitched himself forward through the water curtain to step up into a foothold in the dam, digging in with the sneaker toe. He found a jutting wedge of rock to hang onto and pulled flat against the block and stone. The soft flesh of his fingertips gave on the blunt scar rock, but the water was cold anesthesia. He kept going. Close to the top, he grabbed a tangle of thick root and pulled. His arms tensed and drew him upward and there was pleasure in that feeling of strength when he finally yanked himself up onto the wet narrow tip of the dam.

"Goddamn right!" he shouted as he staggered to the side of the stream. He sprawled out shivering wet in the muddy grass. Sun fell across his legs. The sweet clover smell and the rush of water over the dam worked a calm deep into his bones. For a moment, he almost felt joyous.

He rested for a short while, and then he sat up. He heard his name.

He stood, stepped carefully onto the narrow peak of the dam.

Toward the middle of the dam there was a wood platform jerry-built on top of a cinder-block foundation. It was a few yards wide and a foot higher than the rest of the dam.

It was like stepping up into thin air. Water rushed below and poured out the other side down a churning curtain to the rocks.

After a couple of minutes he squatted down, sat back hard. He let his legs hang in the spray. Cold dampness rose up his seat and bare back.

"Drew!"

Squinting, he looked out at the blue-white sky. Fat clouds ringed the sun and began to form a face. Drew watched the brown eyes smudge with eyeliner. He watched the oval birth mark rise on the cheek.

It was Allison Myers. Her dark hair was cut in a chin bob and her lips were parted to show just the top two teeth.

Drew blinked slowly, and, when he looked at the sun again from the cold-water dam, he saw Allison's face on fire. Her eyes burned. A black ring charred the skin around her eyes. Viscous red bubbles popped one by one at the center of her parted lips before a trickle of black oil pulsed out of her mouth and dripped down her chin.

He heard his name again.

The voice seemed to plunge from the sky. Closer. Louder. That was a dead voice he heard, ringing from Allison's bloody mouth.

24

His name rang across the roaring water. He opened his eyes to see silver spray, a metal net rising toward him. He pulled his wet feet up onto the wood platform and slowly stood.

"Drew!"

The voice was so hoarse he couldn't tell who it was.

He made his hand into a visor, shielding his eyes, and looked in the direction of the house.

It was Bahar.

The specter of her, the way she looked last night, kindled in his memory.

Make it go away.

He saw her with the cop, holding him, whispering in his ear.

Go away.

He saw her face floating over his. He felt the wet grass soak through his pants as she petted his face.

Sshh, sshh, quiet Drew.

He saw her getting into the cop car, leaving him behind.

It's not the way you think it is, Drew.

Now he watched her run to the edge of the lawn and stop. She waved a long arm at him, swaying back and forth.

"Can I come talk to you?" she called. "Please, Drew."

He didn't trust himself to answer, so he stayed quiet.

She ran across the street. She disappeared behind the mill on her way toward him. A black pickup passed on Redder's Road.

Drew pinched the soft skin on the inside of his wrist. He had to keep reminding himself that he hadn't listened to Bahar's story yet. If he wanted to hear it, he'd have to choose his questions as if he couldn't make even one mistake. But to push his mind through the maze of suspicions, with smart rapid intent, was going to milk his reserves, or what was left of them. And on top of that, he had to tamp down his heart's fucking fury. Bahar was *going* to answer a series of questions, and when she was done Drew would know exactly what had happened that night.

Still, this was one dizzying thicket that had grown around his brain overnight: Had Bahar known all along? Of course she had. Had she helped? Define help. Had she gone over to Allison's house that morning? No. The newspapers didn't mention her. They didn't locate her blood at the scene. Had she helped after the fact? Had she put up an alibi? *Get to Jake. You can't hide from Jake. Jake tried to confess*. But to what? What had Jake confessed to? He hadn't really come out and said the words. He'd stopped himself. *But he did take some kind of responsibility. He took a step*. And Bahar kept this a secret for two full years. She pushed me to date him. She lied all the time. *But not to you*. She lied to me about Troy Starr. She had me believing she was pregnant with Arnie's baby. Why that lie? Who gained from it? When she saw Jake in jail, how hard was that? What had she done to make sure he went free? Who had she known? What if she had known cops even back then, even when she was just a girly? *She'd do anything for you, Drew*. She'd do anything for Jake. She'd clean up his car. She'd throw evidence in the river. She'd burn it, bury it, liquefy it in acid. *She'd do anything for you*. She'd do it for Troy Starr. Bahar would do anything.

Drew needed a strong scythe. He patted his hunger-tight belly as blood hummed in his ears and thick veins rose on the tops of his hands. He rehearsed the questions he planned to ask her.

Don't let her dissolve. Don't let her hesitate.

He found himself almost hopping from foot to foot, waiting on a sparring partner.

Come to me baby. Come on Bahar.

And then she did just that. She broke into a run up the grass hill, got a handful of old tree roots, and pulled herself onto the dam. She tripped splashing across the top, climbed into the wooden platform, and came right up beside Drew without taking her eyes off his. She wore a white T-shirt, tight brown pants and flip-flops and an O's cap. A groove between her eyes made her look angry, but otherwise she had the perfectly rested face of a vacationing heiress.

His teeth were clamped. His neck and shoulders were tensed. A charge went down his arms, and when he looked at his hands they had knotted into fists and her lip was split open, bleeding. He looked at the blood on his knuckles and then looked up at her, smiling. A sensation like pinpricks ran up his neck into his face.

"How could you let me be with him?" he spat. "You cunt."

"I've wanted to tell you for so long," she said. "So long." A single tear formed in the corner of her eye. She blinked. The tear disappeared. She held her palm to her mouth.

Drew waited. He just watched her.

Bahar frowned, reached out her hand as if to touch his arm. A band of wavelengths seemed to repel her fingers, and she pulled an inch at a time back from him until her hand was safely returned to her personal space. She flexed it as if to reassure herself how it worked. She looked up at Drew. "You have to let me explain."

He leaned against the wood platform railing and looked at the roaring breakers below. "Has any of it been real, Bahar? Any of it at all?"

"What?" she whispered.

"The way I thought you loved me."

"Yes. All of it."

He turned to look at her. "But you let me love your brother."

"I wanted to tell you."

"Why didn't you tell me before? Why not last night?"

"You're in*ter*rogating me. I couldn't tell you."

He shook his head.

"I had to find Troy," she said. "Drew, you saw him last night all fucked up. Using. I had to find him. He relies on me."

Drew raised an eyebrow.

"And that cop was a good person. He's a very lonely guy."

Again, Drew raised an eyebrow.

"I needed his help." Something flickered in her eyes. She was thinking of a way to break through to him. Drew knew how her brain was wired. "I knew you'd be fine. I didn't know that Troy would. I had to find Troy. I couldn't lose him." She paused, looked away. A long moment passed as Drew watched her watch the water. The silver net billowed up from the rocks below.

She turned to look at him, and when she opened her mouth Drew knew what she was going to tell him. "I know what Arnie told you."

He nodded.

"He left me a furious message. What did he say?"

Drew shook his head no.

"Talk to me. Quit this miming."

He kept his eyes on hers, like he could stay large inside her head, like he could stop her from thinking about anyone else. "Now that I know it's not Arnie's baby," he said, "don't you think that you could tell me whose it is?"

Bahar huffed. She wiped loose strands of hair off her face. A light grew in her eyes and she moved closer to Drew, holding up an open hand, pointing the open fingers at his neck. "You can't merge these different things, Drew. One thing at a time."

He shrugged.

"I want to tell you it all. I wanted to all along, but it was *not* my right. It was *not* my story to tell. And how much should you have to listen to? Do you really want to know just how she died? I won't talk you through the details. I won't. But I want you really to know how Jake got arrested and how it felt to see him in prison and why I couldn't tell you about it until he went first. I wanted you to understand us first—as people. And I want you to hear us explain who Allison was, how we lived together, how the four of us fused, how when she died . . ."

"It was like a part of you died?" Drew asked, smiling. He had had a suspicion that he'd have to ask this question. He watched as she blinked away more tears, and then he asked, "Was that the best you could do for your good friend Allison?"

"What the fuck is this? Drew? I thought . . . Jake said you had a rough time, but . . . but he said you understood."

"Didn't he tell you that he gave me an envelope of news clips to read while he cowered in his bedroom?"

She shook her head slowly. The crease between her eyes sharpened. "No, he didn't," she said. "Jake didn't do that."

Drew nodded.

Then, as if she was talking to herself, she murmured, "Why is he lying to me? Why'd he do that to me?"

"Bahar, shut *up*. I don't *care* about what happened to

you. You kept this from me. I don't *care* how much you missed Allison."

"You don't know what you're saying. My God, you're lumping me in with Jake. That's wrong."

"Is it? You think Allison would agree?"

"If you think fucking with my head is really a way to respect Allie's memory, you're wrong. If you have some delusion that maybe you'll take me to a place I haven't ever gone before, you're wrong as hell. I've blamed myself for every shitty thing I ever did, but I had nothing to do with Allie's murder. And neither did Jake. And neither did Troy."

It was like his heart was a fist that wanted to leap from his mouth, but he made himself stay cool. "Where's your dignity, Bahar? Wanna turn this around on me? That girl's dead and everything *does* point to your brother and your junkie-ass loser friend. The cop, I guess, saved Jake's life. He'd be on death row if it weren't for a sloppy, overeager cop. Guess Jake was just *born* lucky. So why are you still lying to me?"

She staggered a step back from the platform's edge, as if the urge to leap had just shuddered through her. "It was a frame-up. I know how bad it looked, but it was a frame-up."

She had no idea that her brother had all but confessed to him—confessed and said he'd done it for her.

It took Drew a moment to recover. "Why?" he asked unsteadily. "Why did the cop frame him?"

"They raped her. The cops raped her. And they framed Jake and Troy to cover it up."

Drew shook his head. "Why are you still lying to me?"

She stood there, smiling with rage, and said, "You can ask me anything. I have nothing to hide."

"Okay," Drew said. "How did your mom react when she found out that Allison was dead? The way Jake told it, they were as close as mother and daughter."

Bahar shrugged. "They got along. She was Mommy's star patient—three times a week. They had a lot to talk about."

"Why are you still lying?"

"Don't fuck me up, Drew."

"You let me go to bed with Jake, knowing what you know."

"I had no power over that."

Drew shook his head. "Tell me about Troy. He's innocent, too?"

"You don't know Troy."

"Tell me about Arnie. Tell me about Arnie as your baby's dad. Tell me that."

"I can't talk about that now."

Drew pulled in a deep breath, looked across the street. In an oval of bright sun, the house looked even more like a movie set, a housefront built to double-scale in a grove of towering lithe oak and pine trees with foam-rubber trunks. "This is too hard."

Bahar nodded but didn't say anything.

"Is it Troy's baby?"

"I can't talk about it."

"Is it my baby?"

"Drew . . ."

The newspaper stories were coming back to Drew now, in waves: evidence, arguments, testimony, photos. "When Allison was murdered—were you and Troy sleeping together back then?"

"Yes," she said.

"Did Jake kill Allison?"

"No."

"Did Jake kill Allison?" he asked again.

"I will never say that my brother is a murderer. My brother'd never say that I was a murderer. You'd never say that your brother is a murderer. And I know that Ty would always stand by you. So it won't do you any good to ask that question again."

"Why would the cops frame them?"

"I don't know what you want me to say."

Drew wiped his eyes roughly. "Troy didn't drive to Allison's? That morning? To kill her?"

"No."

"Jake didn't either?"

"No."

"And the witnesses who said it was? Were they lying?"

"Or they were just mistaken," she said.

"And the blood that matched Jake and Troy was from some other time that they bled in her house?"

Bahar nodded darkly. "Or it was planted."

He could see now that all of the times he'd fucking foolishly thought his heart was sore, all the times he'd felt bigger than someone, protective—they were nothing. He'd never been a real defender. Now, right now, he knew what pity was.

Drew watched four ducks saunter to the stream bank, flapping, huddling. One by one they stepped onto the water and skimmed along the edge of the waterfall surf. "Who do I look like, Bahar? Allie? Is that who your junkie friend was talking about last night?"

"You look exactly like her, Drew."

He fell silent, but he couldn't bring the girl's face in true focus. "I was hoping you wouldn't say that."

"It's true." She looked away from him. "Let me tell you something else on that subject."

"Go. Tell me."

"When I first saw you," Bahar said evenly, "it almost made me throw up. How much you looked like her. Do you remember how fucked up I seemed when I introduced myself to you? Drew, you could truly be her brother. It might sound awful, but I would've never met you otherwise. How would I have met you? Baby, you were so shy. Remember? You weren't going to meet anybody. Not you."

"Yes, I remember."

"I followed you because you looked like Allie. I made us meet up and then I fell in love with you."

"I don't wanna hear that."

"I loved you before Jake did. I've loved you longer. And I've got your baby, Drew."

There, he thought, she's said it. She's laid her claim.

"I'm the one who wanted to tell you right away. But no way he would let me. He had to go first. He's my brother. I had to protect him."

Drew grabbed her by the shoulders and brought her face closer to his. "How could you wait? If you couldn't tell me, you could've made him." Their faces came together, nose to nose. His breath was short. High old trees swayed green in his side vision and the dam shook with smooth watery sound.

She closed her eyes. "I did make him tell. That's how come it happened at all. Because I made him. You know what I had to do. If it was *your* brother . . . But I see you hate me anyway."

"I want to hate you," Drew said. "I want to leave. I want the whole thing to go away like I never met you. And I don't trust you and I don't believe that you'd fight for me, but I can't help it: I don't hate you." Drew let go of her. "That's where you're wrong. I wouldn't be here if I hated you."

She folded against him, plucking at his arms until he wrapped her in a tight embrace. Her ballcap fell off, churned to the rocky bottom. Drew kissed the top of her head. He kissed her on the tip of her nose. He was crying. "I could never hate you. It like nearly broke my heart to think of what you've been through, living through this with Jake. But that girl's still dead, and there's an absolute limit to what I can give you. I don't have the power that like God has. Just because I feel sad for you doesn't mean you did the right thing. You did what you did. Maybe I would've done it. I don't know. But fuck, it's got to be ended. You have to stop. You can't protect them anymore. They killed her, Bahar. You didn't."

She pulled her head away and looked him close in the eyes. As she petted his face, she said, "I've known since the day I met you that you were going to be my best friend. I was gonna make it work no matter what. But baby, you're wrong. Drew, they didn't do it. I swear to you, Drew, Jake and Troy didn't kill Allison."

Drew shook his head. He could hardly bring himself to say the words. He swallowed hard. "He *told* me. Do you hear me, Bahar? Jake told me he was the killer. He confessed. Not outright. Not all the way, but he was close."

Her eyes rounded out and blackened like buttons. She slumped against the railing.

"He *told* me."

Bahar spoke softly, as if to herself. "If they did it, you'll have to stop me from killing both of them. If they killed my Allie like that..."

Drew stepped back from her. "You know they did it, too. You'd have to know it, too."

She blinked slowly at him. "No, Drew. I swear to you..."

"You need me here, Bahar," he said. "You do. But it's like so lethal for you to give up. It's over. They killed her."

"I swear to you they didn't," she said.

"You don't know how bad I want to believe you."

Drew stepped off the platform and ran, hard, along the top of the dam to the mill side of the stream, down the hilly path, onto the marshy shallows. He kept going along the side of the mill, and he didn't answer her calls. He was afraid to turn and look at her. When he made it around to the front of the mill, air leaked out of him, and he slumped against the door.

25

Weak sun broke against the bottle-glass windows. It felt like the bottom of a well, here inside the stone mill. Dank air hung in dusty layers. Sound barely pushed through the thick walls. Puddles seeped in the corners of the mud floor. Slag water dripped onto an unstable pile of sheet metal back in the shadows, where Drew stood against the damp wall.

He knew that there were reasons to be alone, contemplating an act. There was a time for living in your head, building your will. But you had to know when to switch to action. If you waited just a minute too long, your chance disappeared. This life wanted battle. This life wanted now.

The thing he had to figure out was his loyalty. Who'd he owe? Did he owe Allison Myers? The girl he'd never met? Did he owe her? Was *he* the one who owed her? Or did he owe Bahar? Or Jake? And if he owed all three of them, then what? But what could he do, a weak boy hiding in the dark? It wasn't enough that he wanted to do hard work, that he wanted to do the right thing. It wasn't enough, just to want. Fuck if it ever *had* been. He had stayed here for a reason—a real, hard reason that lurked in the back of his head, hidden away, beyond his reach. All he knew was that he was needed. Needed like he never had been before. He could feel the power deep in his blood.

And he was staying here to use this power. To help them, these awful people he just couldn't stop loving even as they dissolved before his eyes. Now he was strong, stronger, and they were dying. It felt like he had the power to keep them alive. His heart thudded solid in his chest.

The wood door creaked open. Bahar stepped in, head ducked. As she moved slowly to the center of the mill, a wedge of sun lit her from behind.

"Where are you?" she said. "Drew?"

He leaned his face out into the brighter air. "I'm here."

Her breath whistled down her throat like asthma, and she had her feet planted as if she expected a strong wind. "I have to tell you something," she said hoarsely. "You have to listen to me, Drew. Allie was the best friend I ever had before you. She led me to you Drew."

"I *want* to listen," Drew said. He stepped out of the dark. "I want to understand."

Bahar made her hands into one big fist and watched Drew's lip in the half-light. "Because all you see is a dead girl, and that's not who Allie is. Fuck, she beat the hell out of whoever it was. I guarantee you that. She was strong. She was proud. Allie'd run her bike fifteen miles to visit rather than call us and ask for a ride here." Bahar lifted her eyes to meet Drew's. "You don't even know how we met, do you? Her mom used to clean for us—on Wednesdays. Allie helped her after school. That's how I met her. God, she had me scrubbing the shower with Tilex, holding my breath. Like, we'd be laughing, gagging from the fumes. We were twelve."

"Yes," Drew murmured, "yes."

She hugged herself, backed further into the dark. "If Troy or Jake had killed Allie, *I* would have killed *them*. But they're not guilty. You must listen to me. They might look guilty, but they're *not*. Cops might think they're guilty, but they're not. Everyone in Lancaster might think they're guilty, but they're not. They didn't *do* it. Shc was my best friend. My best friend. She was."

You poor girl. You don't want to believe the truth. You just won't let yourself.

"I would *know*," Bahar said. "I would *have* to know."

"Okay honey," Drew said, stepping toward her. He reached out, tried to touch her.

She pulled away. "Two cops framed Jake and Troy. They went to jail. The assistant DA lost his job. Drew, after this trial, the civil case, it's over. We're free. Forever. God can punish us like he wants to for any of our sins. But that's between us and God. We want you *with* us, Drew. *You* are in our life."

I have to make it stop, Drew said to himself. He took another stride closer. He caught her and wrapped his arms around her, held her to his chest.

"Don't touch me," she whispered. "You don't have to touch me. Okay?"

"You know, all I have ever given away my whole life is what I already knew I'd get back. I fucking computed it all. Love, all of it." He kissed the top of her head. "But if I could, I'd say how I killed Allison. I really would. I'd make it all go away from you."

"Would you?" she whispered.

"Yes."

Bahar unhooked his arms and took a step away from him. In the dim light, she turned a long gaze on him. A slow smile ticked open on her face and she began to nod. "You believe me?"

"I'm right here," he said. "I took the step. I'm here."

"But do you believe me?"

"God," he pleaded, holding out his hands. "I know the truth."

"Don't say that. Don't say it like that."

"*You* don't even believe you," he said. "You can't protect him anymore. That part's over. If you help me, then maybe we can pull him through this. Bahar, he has to do this. He has to start. He'll die if he doesn't. This thing's in motion now. He already told me, Bahar."

"No," she whimpered.

"Yes," Drew said. "He's going back to jail."

She looked at the ground. It was like a spirit passed through her. When she lifted up her face, despair overflowed. At first she was standing there, shoulders slumped, and then without a word she just collapsed. Her hands fluttered at her side; she dropped in a rush to the floor as if a hole had opened beneath her. A desolate short cry broke from her throat. "What do I have to do? What can we do?"

"I want to believe you," he said. "Don't you understand? What if Jake *were* innocent? But I don't think he is."

"I think somewhere in your heart you want him to have done it—you want him to be guilty."

"Why? Why would I want that?"

" 'Cause for once," she whispered, "you won't feel inferior. To Jake. To me. To people you think are better than you. These people you worship."

For a moment, Drew felt like running; the muscles in his legs twitched and he cut his eyes to the open door: weak sun and shadow rolling along bare ground, sloping to the stream. *Maybe she really knows me. Maybe she sees me for who I am. But is that all I am?* He squatted down next to her by sheer force of will. He held her head with his palms. He murmured her name. *That can't be all I am. I've got to be more than that.* "No honey. I don't want him to be guilty of anything."

Bahar sniffled loudly. She pulled herself upright, kneeling. Drew rose up with her.

"I want you to believe me, but you can't," she said, and took in a long wet breath. "The way you're looking at me, it's like you think *I* killed Allie."

Something inside Drew tipped over. Spilled. And it was like a blood transfusion—raw, cleansing. It surprised him that he felt such strong love for her, that it could renew from a secret source deep in him. Wave after wave overcame him. He wanted so badly just to protect her from every bad fucking thing she had ever done.

He reached across to her. He lay his palm on her neck. "Bahar—what are you saying?" he asked slowly. "I don't think *you* would kill her. I never said that. You should *never* have kept it secret, but I *never* said it was you."

She was quiet for a moment, the deep blue air was still. Then she said, "But what if someone said I was there?"

He looked at her face, unable to speak. It was like she'd hit him.

"What if Jake said I was there?"

"No you weren't."

"What if Troy said I was there?"

"You weren't there."

"But what if I was? Would you stand by me?"

"You weren't there," Drew implored.

What if I did it for Bahar? That's what Jake had said to him.

"Bahar?" Drew asked. "You can't say *what if*. Were you there?"

She shook her head. She wouldn't look at him. "You can't let Jake confess. Once he starts, he's not going to stop. He'll spill everything. Drew, I couldn't help Allison. I wish I could have. I couldn't keep the girl alive. I can't go to jail, baby."

"Were you there, Bahar?"

"What if it was Troy?" she said. "If it was all Troy? And not Jake?"

The room tilted around Drew. "Say that again, Bahar."

"You heard me."

"You said *what if*. You have to tell me right now if it really *was* just Troy. You have to tell me right now if you were there."

She shook her head. "I can't tell you anything."

"Bahar, if it was just Troy, then why's Jake falling apart in the house? Why'd they arrest Jake and Troy together? Jake's in it, Bahar. I just don't know how much. And you, too, only I don't know how much."

She seemed to be looking right through him.

He nodded without really seeing her. He slowly rose up to his full height, looking down at her. "I'm going to go outside for one minute. Okay? Okay? Wait here for me? Wait here for me."

She nodded slowly.

"Right back," he said softly.

He staggered out of the mill, pulling the door shut after him as he choked, dry-heaving on the sparse ground.

When he was done, he wiped his mouth with his palm and took a handful of grass, chewed it, spat it out. Hunched on all fours, he kept spitting until he couldn't taste anything. Then he stood up and looked around him.

Night was coming fast. The insect noises murmured in the near background and stars were just barely visible behind the screen of evening sky.

He rubbed grass and gravel from his hands, spit on them until they were wet, and then wiped them clean on his jeans.

As he stood there, he slowly became aware of a voice. A

quiet voice behind him. Inside the mill, urgently whispering. It was the kind of voice he couldn't forget.

He heard Bahar answer. Just a couple of words. Then there was silence.

He stepped away from the mill door. He didn't have it in him. He couldn't face Troy Starr. He took another step toward the road.

You look just like her.

You're just like her.

She's dead.

He took another step. He wanted to shrink.

Why did I think I could do this?

But then he turned around. He pulled open the mill door and a figure—pale, fast, thin—ran through the blue dark, deep into the back of the mill. There was no one else.

It took everything in him not to slam the door shut before he could go inside.

"Bahar?" he called. "Bahar?"

Water pinged down the limestone walls. He heard breathing and he didn't want to go inside, but he made himself take one step. The darkness swallowed him. He held his hands out, trying to see. Then he called for her again.

"Just go," she whispered. "Please, please, please, please . . ."

"I'm not leaving you," he pleaded. "Don't even tell me to. It won't work." *I can fucking love every sinner.*

There was the noise of something metal scraping the wall back in the dark. And then silence again.

For a moment, Drew froze. He tried to see deeper back in the night shadows, but it was no use. He took another step forward, an inch of a step, as softly as he could. He had an engine inside him that kept pushing him forward, pushing him toward her.

"I'm over here," Bahar said. She was right in front of him, a foot away.

He went up to her, beneath the thick bottle-green window, and he wrapped her tight in his arms. He put his forehead against her forehead and said, "I have to know what happened there, baby. Why would they say you were there when Allison died? Why would they? What exactly did you do?" With a soft dipping movement, he leaned his thighs and belly into her. He pinned her against the wall. "Tell me," he said. "I'm right here."

She wouldn't look at him. She wouldn't say anything.

There was a noise behind him, metal on stone. It had gotten a lot closer, and all he wanted to do was turn around, but he had to keep right on top of Bahar until she told him what he had to know. He had to gamble. He had to provoke her.

"Did *you* kill her?" he asked.

"Yes," she whispered.

His throat closed up. Very slowly, he made himself swallow.

"How?" he asked.

"With a knife."

"Did you hold the knife?"

"Yes."

"Look into my eyes and tell me, Bahar. And then I'll believe. I promise."

He could see her whites. He didn't blink.

The gritty scrape of metal rang through the mill.

Drew didn't turn away from Bahar.

She lifted her chin and met his gaze. "Thank you for being my friend," she said, "or trying, anyway." And then her eyes clicked, focused, flickered, looking right past him, and she shouted, "No!"

He braced himself. He thought he might be shot. But he didn't let go of her until she knocked his arms off her.

She shouted, "Don't!"

Drew turned around just in time to see Troy Starr, a few feet behind him, drop a heavy black shovel to the ground and backstep a line to the open door. He made a quick feint into the evening dark and disappeared.

A shudder rose up in Drew. He hugged himself and fell against the cold damp wall.

"I'm so sorry," she whispered.

Drew looked in her direction. She was just a dim outline, the tall figure he knew. "You love that monster, don't you?" he said.

"Like you love me," she said.

He reached out his arms, moved closer to her. "That monster," he said.

"Like me," she said.

He watched her face soften. "You love him enough to claim you killed Allison. Bahar, I don't believe you killed her. I'd believe a lot of things about you, but not that." He took her shoulders in his hands again, held her.

Her eyes opened wide, then wider, and brimmed with tears. "If I had tried harder, she'd be alive." She pushed him away, sobbing, and started to run out of the mill.

Drew caught up to her, took her shoulder. "I promise you I'll be with you the whole way, Bahar, the whole way. You have to clean this up. You can't do this. You can't do this to your baby, or our baby, or yourself. How can you love that monster?"

"How can you love me?"

"Because you're so much like I am," he said. "How could I not love you?"

She stopped. It was like her feet were fastened to the ground, but she couldn't stop shaking, rippling in the dark light, like an angry spirit was trying to break out of her skin. "We were sisters like I never had," she said. "We were blood sisters. We were quite literally blood sisters."

"Yes," Drew said gently.

Bahar leaned against the door. Night insects roared.

"And what happened?" Drew said.

She swallowed loud and shook her head.

"You can tell me what happened."

"I won't say anything bad about her. I won't."

"You can tell how it was," Drew said.

"She changed. Like, subtly at first, but then faster. She got this new sound in her voice. Like she was British. That was first. I mean, people around here, I don't know, they talk a certain way. Pennsylvania Dutch. Dutchie. German.

Whatever. It's around. That's how Allison's mom talked, and Allison had it in her voice, but all of a sudden she just changed into this British voice. And then she started coming over to hang out with my mom, and my mom loved her. My mom would call her just to talk. My mom would do everything the way Allison wanted her to: chocolate cake, or her hair, or flowers on the dinner table. And it was the same with Jake. She like had a mission to become closer and closer to him. He'd buy her things. A dress. A CD. Soon it was like expensive dinners. It was a car. A car, Drew. He bought her a car. And if I walked into the room, she'd do anything to take away the attention. And then she seduced Troy. While I was dating him. Some nights she slept with him right after I did. It was disgusting. But I was more disgusting because, because I knew it, because I knew they were getting together night after night and I never said a thing. I just got madder and madder and quieter and quieter while Allison's transformation continued a fucking astonishing progress. She got taller. She got blonder, and smarter, and fiercer. And she was a wire, in fantastic clothes Mom or Jake or Troy bought for her. Her conversation got brighter, and faster, and sexier. She was changing, and so was I. The better she got, the more see-through I became." She stopped again, rubbed her face, and said, "But then Troy didn't want her anymore. Not in an urgent way. It was like she didn't tantalize him anymore. It made me think he burned out on her. He was back with me, pretty much. I mean, we were solid again. Part of it was her background. She like came from *nothing*. That was part of it. He hated that after a bit. The way she acted like she *wasn't* from nothing. So sometimes Troy, he'd *remind* her. I couldn't stand that. He'd just say stuff to see how far he could go. He called her mom a char bitch once and Allie fucking clocked him. In public. She knocked him to the ground with one punch."

"And he killed her," Drew said somberly.

"You can't bring her back," she said. "You won't make things right by putting us in jail, Drew."

He shook his head slowly back and forth. "Troy really did it. Jake really did it. Didn't they? And you. Were you there, too? Were you? When you ask me to stop Jake, is that for you? Are you really asking for you?"

She peeled her back from the mill door, hand over her crying mouth, and got off to a running start. Her footsteps crackled in a quieting line away from him. Then she stopped, turned to face him. "You be with Jake if you must," she called back to him. "You see him through this if you have to. But you have to *know* that you're killing me. If you let him confess, then I'm dead. And I'm putting it all on you. All of it."

In a stupor, Drew followed, one thudding foot after the next. But he was too slow. The chilling air licked at his bare chest. He got to the side of the road, stopped, and watched the giant house, all lighted up. The yew trees glowed like they'd been dipped in an ointment of blue glass. There was something gold-white deep in the boughs. Something sparkling through the branches.

In the corner of his eye, he saw gold hubcaps glinting in

the light of a security pole. He blinked a couple of times, looking at the front of the truck. It was past the house, just around the low dipping curve of Redder's Road. It was almost hidden from sight, a safe distance away. He thought there was a person in the driver's seat. A brown Lincoln Navigator, brand-new.

A long moment passed. He watched the big truck for a sign and then, cautiously, he started to wave. He just lifted up a hand. He waited. The cold dark road was empty, coated with slick night dew.

The headlights blinked discreetly. One quick blink.

Oh thank God, Drew said to himself. The cavalry's here.

26

He pulled open the passenger door and climbed inside, locking the door behind him. "Oh God, am I glad to see you!" he said, and leaned over to kiss Mary Hong. He held on to her, his palms greedy against the back of her neck.

"I was fucking *worried* about you," she said. "Shit, Drew, I'd have gotten here a lot earlier, but I got lost. Like the last time I visited here I said I'd never come back. This out here is crazy, white-man country. I mean, it's *country* country."

He settled back in his seat and looked at the smooth tan console, the haphazard wad of twenties in the drink holder, the black sandals on the floor between Mary's bare, immaculate feet. "Yeah, I guess I was scared when I called you," he said. His eyes had a bad time focusing.

"Scared? You fucking fell apart on me, baby. I almost got some cops in on this. I *saved* that message."

"I know," he said, shaking his head.

"Your voice *scared* hell out of me."

"I was in a different head," he said carefully.

"Are you gonna tell me what?"

He shook his head, watching out the great wide windshield. An army of yellow butterflies wove through high weeds. Past them, the grass was the color of watermelon shell, just mowed to the edge of the mill. "I want to tell you so bad. As soon as I can, I will. If I promise to tell you, will that be good enough? Because right now, I can't."

"No it's not good enough."

"I won't tell you right now."

She was silent for a while, holding the steering wheel in her loose grip. She tapped her feet on the rubber floor mat. "Will you at least tell me on a scale of one to ten how bad a thing it is?"

He thought it over for a minute. "No."

She let out a loud sigh. "What if I heard?" Then she looked a hole deep into his eyes, frowning. Her chin quivered. She shook an empty pack of Camel Lights, and then leaned across Drew's lap. She found a fresh pack in the glove compartment and lit up. "Don't you remember—at the Ruby Lounge, Drew?" She settled back, taking an endless drag.

He squinted at her. "What?"

"I asked you if you wanted to hear a rumor."

He slowly nodded. "I remember. You heard a rumor about *this*?"

She nodded back at him but didn't say anything.

"Who?" he asked. "Who knew?"

"Roy DeSomething," Mary said. "I hardly know him."

"How did he know?"

"Someone's father in New York. Someone who works at *Dateline NBC*. They're doing a story. All I know is that there was a charge of murder and it was dropped. That's it. I won't ask you to tell a story to me. I mean, under the circumstances it would feel obscene to hear it. Now that I know it's true."

"You can't pass this story on," Drew said. "It's not the kind of story to pass on. Mary, it's still happening, right now."

"I'm not passing it on."

He didn't answer.

"I can see what you're going through, Drew. Are you okay here? Can I do anything? Should I kidnap you back to Baltimore? My *worry* isn't important, but you just *have* to tell me if you've got excess on your head that you can't handle."

"Well fuck," he said, and though he felt at any minute he would start to cry again, he smiled at her instead. "It's more, way, way, way, way more than I can handle."

"But you're still here," she said softly.

"Yeah," he answered, "I can't seem to leave."

"But why? Drew, you don't have to get lost in these miseries. You don't."

"I chose them, Mary. Of all the people I've met, I chose them above everyone else. How can I walk away?"

"What do you think?" she asked. "Do you think Jake did it? I just can't seem to help myself either. I'm sorry."

"You don't have to be. But I'm not answering you."

"Then what can I do for you, Drew? Tell me what you want me to do." She turned and faced out the windshield as if to give him a moment of privacy.

He reached over and put his hand on top of her hand. "Man, it just gives me a lot of strong feelings. Maybe I sound one way now. I don't know how I'm coming across. But you know how to make a guy feel stronger." He squeezed her hand. "Thank you."

"Yeah, I'm your fucking friend," she said.

"I know you are."

"I'm your good goddamned friend."

"Yes you are."

"And don't you forget it."

"Never."

She dropped her forehead to the steering wheel. "Drew, it was a *terrifying* message. What are we gonna do about this? I'm driving home now? Am I just gonna leave you? What can I do?"

"Well, you can't really help here," he said softly. "I mean, I don't see how you can help more than you already have. Just coming here like this."

"Look," she said, and she sat up ramrod straight, lifted both their hands from the steering wheel. "I want to just say a prayer. Would you let me?"

"I'd like that," he said quickly.

"You're not shitting me?"

"No," he said, and he looked over at her, sideways, before he bowed his head with her. Then he closed his eyes, held his breath, waiting. The car smelled like lemon.

She took a deep breath. "Hear my prayer, O Lord, and give ear unto my cry. Hold not thy peace at my tears for I am a stranger to thee as all my fathers were. O spare me so I may recover strength. Amen. Amen."

"Amen," Drew said. He opened his eyes. "What time is it?"

Mary pointed at the clock as she read it out loud. It was nearly past eight, nighttime. "Why?" she asked in a whisper.

He had to go. He drummed his thighs with his fists and looked over at her. "I think I need you on this, Mary. And I have like no right to ask you, but I'll do it anyway."

"Absolutely," she nodded. "What do you want me to do?"

He thought about it for a minute. The thing he was afraid of, the thing he was *most* afraid of, was that when he walked inside to see Jake he would make a mistake, panic, and have no allies. A man without allies had to rely only on himself, and he wasn't such a man. Not yet. He couldn't be his own ally yet.

"Mary," he asked, "do you have a pager?"

"Yes," she nodded gravely. "It's 800-Get-Mary."

"And you've got a cell phone?"

"Yes."

"Okay," he said. "Wait here. Keep your doors locked. Just for you to be here will be so strong for me. Just for me to know how I can get away if I have to."

"Yes," she whispered. "I'll wait right here."

"And you're not afraid?"

She shook her head.

"Um, wish me strength," Drew said, and he jumped from the car without looking at her. He kept his eyes on the front of the house as he walked up the road and then the path to the door. He stopped a few yards away and watched every window at once. Shadows rolled across the whole wall of brick and glass and heavy curtains in the shapes of hands and leaves and long spindly branches. The air hung over his shoulders, murmured into his ears, warned him not to step inside the house. He stood there a moment, listening. What was his role here? What could he do? What could he change? He didn't know, didn't know what he even *should* do. Was he just going to give some little handful of comfort? And to what end? He couldn't hold this; he couldn't keep this a secret. He couldn't help Jake get away. He couldn't condemn him. He couldn't hate him. He couldn't betray him and he couldn't love him anymore. He could never understand him. So what was left? Just fear? Just pity? What a world to make, what a life to make for himself. There had to be more than pitiful fear.

And Bahar. She really had been there? Was there a chance that she helped them kill Allison Myers? Or was it just guilt—guilt, laying a backward trail?

It had gotten to the point where Drew felt like he had been a witness, too. Hell, the way the bloody details sat in his blistering head, he felt like a participant.

With a hard twist of the doorknob, he shoved open the door.

He stood there, looking inside at the dark house, and he knew that he could not afford to think. There was enough fear to be had just from peering across the polished wood floors, room upon room, doors shut, everything quiet, everything in waiting. He paused for a moment, checked his body head to toe, silently, with his jittery mind's eye.

Okay, he told himself, looks like everything's working. Gotta move.

27

The stairs and the staircase were newer than the rest of the house. Each step was half-timbered, with the wood and masonry fitted precisely. They were wide steps with a rugged simple banister jutting along each side. Near the second-floor landing, the stairs flared still wider, slowing you before the gashing fretwork that rose up from the wood floor, up the banister, up up up in the same gothic pattern, a meticulous spray covering the coffered ceiling.

Drew stood there, like he was in a church, face up to see the delicate black grooves. They had the appearance of a broad span of wings. There was a clear bulb recessed in the center; its shadows gave the illusion of flight.

Suddenly, with his neck stretched taut, Drew felt vulnerable. He put his palms flat against his skin, made a collar.

He was standing right in front of Jake's bedroom, and it was time. He pounded twice on the door.

"Come in," Jake called calmly.

Drew hesitated. He looked over his shoulder, down the stairs.

"Come in," Jake said again.

"It's me," Drew said, opening the door and stepping inside.

"Yup, it's you." Jake was shirtless in jeans, barefoot, thick bristle on his cheeks.

"Get off the phone," Drew spat.

Jake held his gaze for a long minute. Then he turned away and talked quietly. As soon as he finished, he threw the phone onto his bed and dropped into the chair beside his desk. He shook his head, looking around at the room. It was in a jumble—books, papers, and clothes strewn from the corners, drawers falling out of the bureau, mattress skewed on the chair. There was a stench like ripe roses. "A big hello from my mother," Jake said.

"I'm sorry about earlier," Drew said. "I was scared."

"Of course you were," Jake said.

"I'm still scared."

Jake nodded. "I killed her," he said. "I killed Allison."

Drew swallowed hard. He nodded. He kept his eyes on Jake, but inside he was running through a nest of questions and orders, ways to get through this moment and then the next and the one after. He was going to stay here in this room until he knew the whole story, until he knew *why*, until he saw Jake standing in front of him, the real Jake he had come to love. That boy still existed; Drew didn't have a doubt. But he was also a killer.

Jake fell back on the chair. "I never said that before today. I mean *never*. Never with Troy. Never with Bahar. Never with lawyers. Never with Mom. Never with Dad. Never until I met you."

You're enough like me that I can trust you.

"Not to your mother?" Drew asked. "Really?"

"Not to her, really. My mother would never let me say it. Not those words. She'd stop me if I tried." He sat up on the bed. "She can hardly stand to look in my face, Drew. And I live here with it every day. How could she love me? I killed that girl and I got off with a few months in jail. I can't even be retried. Troy can't either. Double jeopardy. At least for the murder part. They'll get me some other way. They'll have to."

Drew clasped his shaking hands behind his back. *They got away with it, didn't they? The judge said they can't be retried*. It was all he could do to stay there, facing Jake. Slowly, he squatted to the floor so he was lower than Jake, unthreatening, looking up at him. "What do you want from *me*? Why did you tell *me*? What can I do here?"

Jake leaned forward on his chair. He rested his elbows on his thighs and put his face right in front of Drew's, looked deep into his eyes. "I could still get away with it, if I hadn't told you. I could keep getting away with it for the rest of my life. But now I told you. And you won't let me. I knew you wouldn't let me, Drew."

"What would I do to stop you?"

Jake shook his head and pulled his old wallet out of his

back pocket, flipped it open. "Look at this," he said. "There. There it is."

Drew looked silently at the two photos in their sleeves. In one photo, it was him, smiling, looking right into the camera. And in the other photo, facing it, was Allison. She had the exact same smile. She had the exact same eyes, lips. Her face was softer, rounder, but she could have been Drew's sister. He shut the wallet and pushed it back to Jake, pushed it against his knee. "I have no fucking clue what kind of reaction you expect from me. You have it in your wallet, a picture of the girl you killed."

"I just put it there. Tonight. For when I confess. I tell the whole world tonight, Drew."

Drew's lids fluttered open. "On *Larry King*."

Jake let out a long sigh. He reached out to take Drew's hand. Drew surprised himself and let his hand be held. The hand felt the same way it had felt before. Drew still liked the feel of it.

"Thank you," Jake said.

"Why do you say that? What have I done?"

"You stayed," Jake said.

"I'm gonna stay," Drew said, nodding. "I'm here."

"I know you will."

"I won't leave you." The words hung between them. Though Drew heard the foul implications, he didn't let himself ponder them. *It is time. Now.* He pulled Jake's hand down into his own lap and took a deep breath and asked, "Why?"

Jake just nodded. "Okay," he said. "Okay. Okay." He

nodded as if he didn't understand. "The newspapers had it all wrong. They still don't know what happened."

"Why?"

"Okay, Drew. I heard you."

Drew held his hand tighter. "Why, Jake?"

"There wasn't a plan," he started, and then his face crinkled up and he looked at the ground.

"Why?" Drew asked more insistently.

Jake winced. "Allison had just gotten out of the hospital . . ."

Drew couldn't help filling in: *When you killed her*.

"It was the fourth time she had tried to kill herself," Jake went on. "This time with downs and a bottle of Grey Goose. At the little house."

"The little house?"

"Out there," Jake said, pointing through the window to a line of trees. "Way out there. It's a cabin. One room. Where we used to drink. Party. Like that. It used to be out there."

Drew nodded. An eerie calm had fallen over the room.

"So as soon as Allison got out of the hospital, she came over here and we started drinking right away, here in my room. And then we smoked a joint, and then we got the idea to take some 'shrooms. We were knocked out. We were sixteen. Like I was fifteen, actually. Like I couldn't see right. There wasn't the right kind of depth in my vision or whatever. Allie gave me one of her Depakotes. She put it on her tongue and held it out to me. And I took it. We kissed." For a moment, he looked like he might faint. His head swayed. His black, deep eyes couldn't hold the light.

Drew said, "You should just keep going."

"Yeah, yeah," Jake said. "We stopped kissing. I was like, can we get outta here, I gotta go for a walk. She was happy. She'd had all these great sessions with Mom in the hospital. Mom really fills her patients up. They think they can do anything. So Allie was so, I gotta go, I gotta go, I have to get out of here—saying it all along with me. So we left. We walked over to the stream, but it was cold by the water, so then I said, 'We can take some firewood along, we can go sleep at the little house.' And she was like, 'Sleep?' Then we were at the line of the woods, the edge."

Drew couldn't watch him anymore, so he looked slowly down at his hands.

"So it's about half a mile in the woods, the little house. As we get closer, we see the lights are on, a fire's burning. Allison breaks away from me, runs up to the door, and disappears inside, and the second that the door closes, I hear her start to shout. I like run as well as I can, but I'm so messed up that it takes me longer to get there. I open the door and Bahar and Troy are in there, in bed, making out, and I turn and look at Allison, and she's sitting on a chair, stoned out of her mind, peeling off her jeans, and she goes to me, 'They can't push me away,' in a zombie voice, 'They do it because they think I'll go away.' And then all of a sudden Troy starts making these rude jokes about Allison and her mom in a sort of imitation of her voice, and then he goes like, 'Classy lady, is she a classy lady,' and that starts Bahar up. She starts imitating Allie's mother, the way that she talks, the Pennsylvania Dutch. It hits me then. Just something in their voices."

Drew nodded, eyes on the floor. "Keep going."

"Yeah, yeah, I'll keep going. So they're just ambushing her from both sides, shouting shit at her, laughing at her, ridiculing her. I started to cry, but Allie just looked over at me and said, 'Don't you dare fucking cry for me.' And I stopped cold. And I stood up. And I said, 'Let's go Allie, let's go back to the house.' Allie nodded. She said how she wanted to go hang out with Mom. I tensed up. I knew that was wrong to say. Right then. Bahar was going to incinerate her for that. It was the thing Bahar hated most, even more than Allie with Troy. So I turned around to see what was going to happen next, and that's when wave after wave of fucking Depakote and 'shrooms hit me."

"Right at that moment," Drew said. He pulled his knees toward his chest.

"Yes. All of a sudden I come to, like I've been out cold. I see a flash and it's like everything's different. I see that Allie is in bed with Bahar. See a flash. See Troy taking a photo. I like sit up. Allison's crying, but Bahar's on top of her, poking her and whispering, then touching her and consoling her. Bahar's like, 'No, that didn't happen, no that didn't happen,' and I'm like, 'What is it? What?' and Troy won't look at me, Troy won't answer, so I jump up to my feet and sort of stagger over to the bed and there's like a hundred Polaroids there, and they're of us all, in combinations, making out, getting undressed, me and Allie, me and Troy, Troy and Allie, and I look hard at the photos and I see that Allie's wrists are tied."

Drew had let out a low moan before he could stop himself. "Go on," he whispered.

Jake waited a moment, breathing loudly. "Okay," he said. "Now at this point, it was like I'd sobered up completely. And I look a long time at the photo and then I look over at the real Allie, who is right there on the bed, and I see that she has a cut on her, on her wrist, a shallow cut but it's bleeding. The sheets are covered with her blood. She is dying right there in front of me."

Drew tried to swallow. He worked to keep his head still. From the moment Jake mimicked Allison's mother, talked about how they'd imitated Allison's mother, it was all Drew could do not to throw a hard fist at Jake, slam him face-first into the wall. Hearing this story, he barely saw Allison herself, Allison, a girl separate from him. With each new layer of the story he saw his brother, his mom; he saw himself.

She could be my sister.

She like came from nothing.

"And the whole time they were killing her," Drew said, "where did you say you were? Passed out?"

"No," Jake murmured. "No, no, no, no, no. I don't remember it, but I was there. I was in it. There were photos that prove it. And right then, as I looked down at Allison bleeding, I saw the photos heaped beside her body, and I was in them."

Suddenly, Drew remembered the photo that Troy Starr had wanted to give him, out back of the mill house.

"What did you see in the photos?"

"It all came back to me then. I saw it all in the photos like it was happening right in front of me again. It's like I'm hearing her. She kept saying, 'Don't. Don't. Don't.' Then she said, 'Where am I, where am I?' Then she said, 'You raped me, and I thought you were my friend, you raped me, I thought you were, you raped me you were my friend, my friend raped me.' That's when it all came apart in my head, and I remembered everything."

"You raped her," Drew said, and finally he looked up. He made himself lock eyes with Jake. "You were fucked up and you raped her and then you killed her."

"Troy kept telling me, 'You raped her, your life's over. Jake, you raped her.' And I looked down at the photos and it looked like what he said was true. I mean, I only saw the Polaroids for just a minute. I never saw them again."

"But you thought you had to kill her."

"Troy kept changing what he said."

"He told you that you raped her. What else?"

"Troy said we hadn't raped her. He said she had to die or our lives were over. She'd ruin our lives. She'd say that we'd raped a drunk girl. Troy said, 'You cut her, Jake. You cut her.' Troy said I should cut her. He said, 'You cut her, Jake. You cut her. We can make it look like she killed herself.' He had a thin knife. A thin thin knife. It glinted. I saw five knifes. And he grabbed her arm, lifted it up. He cut her wrist open."

"Stop," Drew said.

Jake shook his head, trapped in story. "I held her down. Held her down. I didn't help her. I held her down. He kept cutting her. 'No one raped you,' he said. 'No one raped you.' I was holding her down and she grabbed my wrist."

Drew winced, and despite himself he brought his hand up to his mouth and sat back from Jake.

"She said, 'Save me.' "

Drew watched him.

"She said, 'Save me.' "

"Why?" Drew asked. "Why?"

Jake screwed up his face and tried to look away, but he kept a tight watch on Drew. "Because we were mad at her," he said. "There wasn't any other reason. Nothing else. We were mad at her and then we killed her."

"And what about Bahar? Where was she?"

"I used to think that was important, too."

"Where was Bahar? I have to know. I have a right to know."

"I never told on her, Drew. I never never will. I can't ever, ever be forgiven for what I did. That's the rest of my life. She's got to come to her own fuckin' conclusion. It's not coming from me. No way."

A gap opened up in Drew's raw brain. He shook his head before he asked, "But the newspaper said they found Allison's body inside her house . . ."

"We took the body there."

"Why?"

"It just happened. We knew exactly when her mom was

going off to work. I thought we were going to get caught. I was sure. And if we got caught here . . . the way my Mom loved Allie . . . I couldn't . . . the body couldn't be here. Me and Troy put it in the trunk. And burned the little house. We got rid of all the evidence."

"Keep going," Drew whispered.

"We were in the middle of the woods. It was nowhere. It was a shack. One room. Thin walls. Built on a cement platform. And so we burned it down to ashes that night."

"And then . . ."

"We loaded Allison's body in Troy's trunk and drove her over there to her house, put her back inside the house."

"Where was Bahar?"

"Here, telling Mom. Putting together the alibi."

"Bahar told her, right then? My God."

Jake looked at the floor, shaking his head. "I can't tell you Bahar's story. I wish you could get through to her. Maybe if you tried, maybe she'd tell you. That would be the first step. But I can't get through to her."

"I've tried," Drew said.

"I know you have. But if you can find it somewhere inside you to try just a little bit harder . . ."

When the doorbell rang, it was like a church bell pealing. It reverberated deep in Drew's chest. He lifted up to his full height and staggered a couple of steps. He was light-headed. He tilted and leaned against the wall, watched Jake pace to the bedroom door and rip it open. A cone of hall light dropped across the floor.

Jake stepped to the top of the stairs and leaned to look down at the front door.

"Who is it?" Drew asked.

A long minute passed in silence as Jake watched downstairs to see who was there. He got up on tip-toe to see better down to the dark front windows.

Finally, he turned around and asked, "So have you met Troy? I believe that's him waiting downstairs."

A cold shudder went through Drew, and, clutching his stomach, he stumbled into the bathroom, threw open the toilet. Sweat ran up his torso. His greasy hair stuck to his head. He stood over the bowl, panting, but nothing came out.

He turned to the gleaming white sink and looked in the mirror at his face. He was haggard, with chin stubble, oily face, nest of matted hair.

A loud thought flashed through his brain like a headache, but he pushed it away. He watched himself in the silver-white light as the thought fought its way back. How could he reason with it? There was no way.

Maybe Jake didn't rape Allison.

Maybe Jake didn't kill Allison.

Maybe it was all Troy Starr. Maybe Troy convinced Jake of it, convinced him that he'd done it.

The Polaroids, Drew thought. The proof was in the photos. And Troy still had them. Drew was sure of it.

This—this was his test. God had brought him to his test.

He held on to the sink, forcing himself to watch his own

eyes staring back at him. Something had happened to him as Jake opened, as Jake confessed to him. It was like something had happened right in his soul. Jake had admitted rape and murder, but still Drew had this love for him. He didn't feel better than Jake. He didn't feel qualified to judge him, condemn him, whatever it was he thought he was supposed to do.

Maybe Jake didn't rape her.

Maybe Jake didn't kill her.

But why couldn't he just accept Jake's confession? Why did he still think that maybe it wasn't true?

He turned on the cold water, ran it hard, cupping palmfuls to his face. He let the water run. He stared at the mirror—only it didn't work like a mirror. He didn't see his reflection. He didn't see anything. He saw blank silver. He saw that hard, cool surface.

He pulled a handful of tissues from a dispenser, soaked them in the cold running water, and pressed them against his eyes. For clarity. The soft chilly wetness spread across his face, and for a moment he disappeared into white nothingness, a blizzard. Safe and alone inside himself.

Then, slowly, he peeled the tissues from his eyes.

He stepped back, dropped the wet wad into the trash can, then started to back out the bathroom door. But the way the dense heavy ball of tissue landed, with a solid thuck, shifted the contents of the trash can, pulled ribbons of toilet paper down with it, like a drain had opened at the can's base, and Drew saw clearly at the bottom, leaking through a red wrapper, a bloody tampon. He looked for a moment before he understood what it meant.

It was still wet.

The blood was fresh.

He stood there, trying to think, but his reeling head stopped hard. *It's not my baby. I'm not the father. It's not mine. There's no baby at all.* He slumped against the wall, sinking. The sound of water running filled his heart.

And then he heard two thumps from downstairs. One right after the next. He hardly hesitated before he ran out into the hall, and then downstairs.

28

Troy Starr was crouched at the foot of the stairs, touching a cut on his face. In a new crisp white shirt, black jeans, lace-ups, and a heavy silver watch, he was a different person than the junky Drew had seen last night. Drew approached him warily; he wanted to beat him. He slowed himself down the final few steps, watching him closely.

"Where's Jake?" Drew said.

"He can't do this," Troy said. "He doesn't have any idea what he's doing. We'll go back to jail." He stood up, wincing. His nose was dripping blood; his lip was split open.

Drew moved up against him, pushed his shoulders tight against the door. "Where's Jake?"

Troy looked at him with cold blue-white eyes, growling, "You don't know what you're doing, either. You won't see him again. It means jail. They will find a way to put him back in jail and I am not going along. Your boyfriend will spend the rest of his life in jail, you idiot piece of shit. Is that what you want? You already in his will?"

Drew put his face right up to Troy's and said, "Tell me where he is." Then he took Troy's wrist in his hand and turned it so he could see the watch clearly.

Troy shook his head wearily. "Look what time it is. It's just about nine."

"Larry King," Drew said, and he let go of Troy. He started to the kitchen, calling for Jake at the top of his voice.

"I'm here," Jake answered quietly from the barroom.

Drew looked straight down the hallway. He saw the big TV in the dark. A commercial for Advil played. He moved slowly closer to the flickering screen. His footsteps clicked across the heavy wood.

He was almost there when the wall phone rang beside his head, and he instinctively reached for it. "Hello?" At the moment he spoke, he heard the front door slam shut. He turned slowly around, looked back into the kitchen, into the front hall. The rooms were empty. Troy Starr was gone.

He stood perfectly still.

"Hello, Drew," Tamar said breathlessly. "Is everything okay?"

He didn't answer right away, and then, loudly, he said, "Hey, Tamar." He turned back to the barroom, where the TV blared on, a commercial for the Acura Vigor. He watched the empty room, holding his breath, until Jake's face appeared. Jake shook his head slowly back and forth and mouthed the word "no." He made a Don't Enter sign with his hands, palms facing out.

"Tamar," Drew said, "everything's under control."

"Let me talk to Jake," she said. "He hasn't checked in yet."

"Um . . ."

"Drew, I'm about to go on the air. Put Jake on. He's supposed to have checked in with his lawyer. His lawyer's waiting for him."

"Tamar, he can't talk right now."

There was silence. Drew leaned forward, on tip-toes, to watch around the corner where Jake stood, remote control in hand.

An ad soothed the TV screen, an ad for the Berck-Plage, the glittering hotel, all shadows, a calm green sea, a pale pale drape flapping out an open window, candles on a table, bouquets of round, fat lime leaves.

Suddenly, the volume rose, just in time for Drew to hear a man speak in crisp British tones: "This. This must be where you belong in the world. Here. The Berck-Plage."

Drew was aware of Tamar's voice in his ear. She asked, "What's wrong?" She said, "Please, please. Let me talk to Jake."

"I can't," Drew said quietly, and he hung up.

He went into the barroom. Jake sat on a barstool, watching as the *Larry King Live* logo filled the screen. Jake smiled grimly.

On TV, Larry King said, "This case has just started to draw attention, but it's a fascinating story."

A thrill kindled up Drew's legs.

The phone rang. Neither of them moved to answer it.

Larry King gave background. It was like reading the newspaper clips all over again.

Then he disappeared from the screen. Tamar took his spot and, behind her, studio lights sparkled.

Larry King bobbed his head at Tamar.

The phone stopped ringing.

Tamar wore a black Prada jacket over a halter. She wore matte makeup, blackberry lipstick. Her long curly hair was done up in an elegant knot.

Larry King didn't fuck around. After giving background, after listing Tamar's credentials and naming her books, he said, "Allie. Allison Myers. Tell me about her."

The words were slow, slurred in Drew's perception, and he was barely able to turn and look at Jake. "Does your mom have any idea what's going to happen tonight?"

"No," Jake said softly. "How could I tell her? Her life's not gonna come back to her."

"Allison Myers was a devastatingly lovely young woman," Tamar said. "She had a fierce intelligence. She was one of my patients, but I also thought of her as a friend. She was just coming into a new phase in her life. She was learning what kind of powerfully aggressive woman she could be." Tamar paused for a moment, and the camera moved closer to her. She took a long slow drink of water as she wiped tears from her eyes. "In 1993," she continued, "on that cold winter morning, Allie was brutally murdered.

My son, Jake, who had been a friend of Allie's, was arrested for the murder. But he was innocent. All charges were dismissed. Now there's only this—an ill-advised civil suit brought by Allison's mother. She cannot win."

"How much is the suit?" Larry King asked.

"Ten and a half million dollars."

"Lot of money."

"We don't have that kind of money, Larry. It's ruinous and it is malicious."

Drew looked over at Jake's taut profile.

"We'll take a break here," Larry King said in somber voice.

Adam Sandler's face leered across the screen.

Jake turned to Drew, tears leaking down his cheeks, and said, "Find Bahar, Drew. Please. She has to do this, too. I want her to, with me."

"I tried," Drew said. "But she ran away."

"Find her. Please."

"What can I tell her? You have to help me."

Jake's face pinched up and he looked away for a moment. Then, when he turned back, he said, "Tell her I tried to protect her, but I couldn't do it anymore. Tell her I have to tell the truth and I want her to tell the truth, too."

That means it's up to me. I've got to convince her.

Drew started to talk but Jake blurted over him: "I'm gonna do it anyway. I can do it alone."

Drew wrapped him in a tight hug and kissed his cheek. "You're going to be better for this. You're strong. You've got dignity. It will last you your whole life. I believe that."

"I'm going to jail for the rest of my life, aren't I?"

Drew nodded against Jake's face. "I think you are."

"I knew that."

Drew murmured his name.

"Thank you for loving me," Jake whispered. "For the time that I have left."

Drew stopped breathing. He looked at the TV. He looked over at the mantle clock. It was already nine after nine. "You're going to make it. Okay? You're going to make it. I'm going to find Bahar now. I'm gonna help her make things right."

Jake smiled, lopsided. "Thank you," he said. "Thank you." His eyes drifted from Drew's face back to the TV, to returning Larry King. He watched the TV screen, suddenly panting and forlorn and dazzled by what he was about to do.

29

Drew ran hard up Redder's Road. It was a dark night with just the moon to see by. Breath came shallow as he kept running, and he slowed to a stop.

He stood at the side of the road beside the spot where Mary had been parked. She was gone.

A car tore past, lights off. Crisp synthetic music rolled out the windows.

Drew watched as the street emptied again, glistening, moonlit like a pond. Knotted dark branches shook in the breeze, and for as far as Drew could see there was nothing but green-black road, tree and sky.

Then he saw taillights. The Navigator, parked nose-in further down Redder's Road, on the stream side of the road. Steam emanated from the back tires.

His feet clapped hard as he raced to the car, knocking on the windows and frame, up the long length to her window. He called her name over and over in a soothing voice, like he was afraid that he might not find her there.

Like Troy had gotten to her first.

Or Bahar.

He pushed his face up against the dark glass.

Her window rolled down. "I had to move," she said. "He's live on the radio, Drew. Some local station's doing a simulcast."

Drew stuck his head in the car with her and listened. "Has he said it yet?"

Mary turned. Her face was just inches from his and he saw the clear shock light on her face. "Oh my God," she said. "He's really gonna confess?"

"Yes," Drew said.

They both quieted, and Larry King's voice filled the air. "Is it fair to say that you and Allison were good friends?" he asked.

"Yes," Jake said. His voice sounded like a little boy's.

Drew shook his head. "I've got to find Bahar."

"I saw a car go up in there." Mary pushed Drew's head outside the car and pointed across the street at the woods. "A BMW."

Drew let his eyes adjust to the shimmering trees. Cautiously, he made out the gaping black hole, the hint of a dirt road. Maybe, he thought. Maybe that's a road.

Larry King said, "Hold on. We've got a surprise call."

"Can I use your truck?" Drew asked Mary.

"Yes," she said. "I'll go with you."

"Mary, I want to ask you to do something else."

"Anything."

"I'm worried about Jake. I want to drop you off, right behind the house. You can watch in the back window. If you see something, like Jake looks like he's going to do something fucked up, like he might kill himself, just call 911 on your cell."

She chewed her bottom lip. "Drew, I'll do it, but why don't I just call now? Why take a risk?"

"Because if he doesn't get his chance, his chance to confess, then he might as well be dead."

Mary nodded sharply. "I'll do my best," she said. "I will not fuck this up."

"Neither will I," Drew said.

30

The Navigator bucked headlong through the black forest. Trees passed the windows, bleached like bones and then dark again. *Where am I going? Where does this take you?* The road lay straight before him; his spilled headlights pulled it beneath the truck.

On the radio, Troy Starr whimpered pitifully. He told a story like Jake's to Larry King. Piece of a story.

Drew heard Jake's voice sighing in relief and agreement. That was Tamar's voice crying, Larry King containing his excitement.

Bahar, now's your chance. Let it out.

Troy Starr said, "I was afraid." He said, "Yes I raped her it didn't start as a rape she didn't say No until I was inside of her and I couldn't stop and then she said No and then she said Stop. I didn't stop. We were messed up. I didn't know what happened. There was a knife. Jake had a sharp little thin knife . . . And we cut her."

Jake's knife? Jake had a sharp little thin knife . . . When would Jake tell his story? Jake was just there, fucked up on drugs. Jake didn't bring a knife. That's not who Jake is.

The road was sloppy mud now. Rocks popped under the tires and pinged against the truck body. The Navigator bounced and lifted up and flew a couple yards before landing hard. As headlights jostled deeper and deeper, illuminating clearings and sharp furrows, there was a split second where Drew glimpsed a pale white face running a crooked path through the woods. He slammed the brakes, checking in the rearview mirror. A dark stillness poured toward him from deep in the trees, but he kept watching until all he saw was the silver-black glass. Nothing.

And then the face appeared again, closer, right along the side of the road.

Bahar.

He kept watch in the rearview and pushed his foot heavier on the gas, thundering backward, bumping hard over the dirt road.

She started to run again, so he could only see her fleetingly among the trees, her hair and then her shoulders flashing in a fog of moonlight.

Suddenly, there was a thick silence on the radio.

"Troy?" Larry King asked. "Troy?"

More silence.

Drew shoved the Navigator into Drive and thundered forward.

"Larry?" Jake said on the radio. "What Troy just told you is the truth."

Tamar started to protest, but then her voice fizzled away.

No. You're not going to say that. Don't. Not that.

"I raped Allison," Jake said.

You raped Allison.

"I had the knife," Jake said.

You had the knife.

"I killed her, too," Jake said.

The Navigator headlights swung over glinting metal hubcaps.

Troy's BMW. Parked on top of a cement platform. The foundation, all that remained of the little house where they'd killed Allison.

Drew skidded up beside it, and as he shifted into Park he saw out of his side vision that Troy Starr had shot himself dead.

He came around the front of the BMW to Troy's body slumped in the driver's seat, over the steering wheel. There was blood on his hand, where it lay in his lap, and a rough red plug on the side of his head. His eyes were open. As Drew reached in to close them, he heard a tiny whirring voice. He looked across to the other seat; a cell phone sat there, live, still connected to *Larry King Live*.

Drew went to the other door and picked up the phone, switched it off. *Enough. That's all for you.*

Then he saw them. The shoebox of Polaroids. On the backseat.

Evidence. Documentary evidence.

The crime in process.

He opened the back door and reached in for the box, pulled it out, and held it in front of him without looking down at the photos until he dropped the box. It landed at his feet, on uneven ground, and as he knelt to gather the scattered Polaroids they appeared to catch fire, layer by layer. They seemed to melt, smoking over, one after the next. An image would glimmer in front of his eyes—the naked body, the face, Jake, Bahar, Troy, Allison, the insides of a shanty cabin—and then the photo would flare up. Masses of seven or eight photos would clump together before flaring to charcoal.

But there was no fire.

The photos weren't burning.

And they weren't crime-scene shots.

Drew tipped the box on its side and fanned out the Polaroids, flipping rapid-fire past each smiling face, each smooth chest and strong back.

These were just snapshots. Keepsakes. Candids.

Just a box of old photos, old friends.

When he finished checking every last image, Drew put them all back in the shoebox and slid it onto the seat where he'd found it. He climbed into the passenger seat and reached gingerly for Troy's neck.

No pulse.

"Hear my prayer, O Lord," Drew begged in a quiet voice. "Give ear unto my cry."

31

The edge of the woods gaped before him, flashing along a line where it became lawn. The high security lights flared at his arrival. Branches came out of nowhere, slapping his face and chest and belly.

He slowed down at the edge of the pool and walked warily next to the house.

He stopped at the widest back window, where the bar-room stuck out from the rest of the house, and looked inside.

Jake sat on the floor. Mary Hong knelt beside him, holding on to him. She met Drew's gaze and shook her head sadly. Jake did not look up.

Drew leaned his forehead to the glass, kept it there a moment to watch Jake; then he stepped away. *You're lost to me. You're not here anymore*. He looked down at himself. He was covered in sweaty grime, shirtless, stomach shriveled tight from hunger. As security lights blasted in the trees, his skin changed from blue to bleach-white and back again to blue.

He turned away from the house, slowly at first, and then fast as his heart beat the pace. He ran faster, pushing around the side of the big house, slipping across the dewy grass, down to Redder's Road. He rounded the mill, and that's where he found her, halfway up the slope to the dam.

He took a couple of soft steps closer, sidling up against the stone wall.

"Who's there?" she called out.

He held himself tight and still in the night shadows.

"Drew?" she said. "Drew, is it you?"

He didn't answer.

"I'm glad if it's you," she called, with a note of fear sharp in her voice.

Still he didn't answer, but watched her take a step down onto lower ground.

"Troy?" she said, and now she sounded a little bit happier, a little bit less afraid.

Cold slicked Drew's insides, hollowed out his stomach. All he wanted to do was fall to his knees, go unconscious.

"Troy?" she whispered. "Is that you?" She paced down to where Drew stood and hesitated when she saw it was him.

Drew stepped out of the dark, and for a moment he wasn't sure what he would say. He thought he had one chance to get her honest, so at the last minute he came up to her and took her shoulders and pulled her against him.

"Troy confessed," he said. "Honey, that is the only thing he could do."

He watched her to see if she already knew.

Her face flinched away from him like he'd punched her. *No, she didn't know. No, she must not have heard it. No, she must be waiting, hiding until the night ends.*

Part of Drew wanted to let her wait through the night, just a final night where she could pretend to be someone else, someone in a different life, someone who had really loved her friend Allison, loved and protected her when two guys raped her, when two guys had a knife. Because if she had, there might be a person worth saving, and maybe this cold light wouldn't be creeping up Drew's legs, up, up into his chest, chilling his heart.

But how could he give her that innocent night? How could he? How could he give *himself* that—a lie, as if the only thing that mattered was what *he* wanted, how much *he* loved her, had once loved her. Big love. As if it protected you.

"The police are on their way," he told her now, still holding her tight to his chest. "It's over, Bahar. Jake 'n' Troy confessed. It's *over*. You have to tell your part. Do it now. Your mother, she broke down, too." Now Drew was risking it all, anything, any shape of the truth that might make Bahar come clean. "Tamar started telling her story on TV. Honey, you have to do it. I'll go with you, baby. I'll be there the whole time, I swear."

"Drew?" she sniffled.

"What?"

"How can you still be like this to me?"

"Because I still love you."

"Is that true?"

"Yeah, I do," he murmured. "But it's the saddest feeling. It feels like the end of something. Well, it *is* the end of something. You know that. Fuck, honey, you've always known it—haven't you, honey? Tell me the truth. Just this once. From the first time you met me, you knew that one day it would end like this. A sad black end."

"Yes," she whispered into his chest. "I always knew."

"You killed Allison," Drew whispered. "As much as Troy. Just as much as Jake did. You're going to jail, Bahar. I'm going to be there. I'll visit you. But you also have to know I'll testify for the prosecution."

She struggled in his embrace, crying softly.

"I'll do whatever I have to, Bahar. You have to pay." He put his lips on her forehead, held them there, but he didn't kiss her. He was crying now, too. "You have to be ready for that."

"But I'm not," she said.

"Your time has run out. You have to know that."

"I don't."

"Bahar," he said. "Bahar, it's over."

She wriggled out of his arms, pulled away. "Then how can you ask me to turn myself in? I'd rather be dead than do that. That's not life, Drew." She started running up the hill to the dam. Drew watched her, and he knew her intentions. She wanted to die. Right at this moment, she wanted to die. Her feet planted hard into the muddy upslope as she ran to the peak without slipping.

Before he knew what he was doing, Drew was starting up after her, catching up to her by pure will. His footsteps had a slapping rhythm, *thwack thwack*, following her, and then he fell. His knee landed flat against a rock and pain burned up his thigh. He looked up to see her crest the dam. She stood looking down the face of the waterfall. Drew heard it roaring beneath her. He took a painful few seconds to get up on his feet and start climbing up toward her. He needed time.

"Troy beat you to it!" he shouted. "He already shot himself!"

She whipped her head around to look in his direction. "What? Drew, what did you say?" She looked down into the water again, a long moment as he kept climbing toward her.

Finally, he was almost beside her on top of the dam. Surging green-black water pounded the rocks below. He inched closer, not looking at her. *Keep it calm. Keep it slack.* When he was next to her, he slowly lifted his arm around her shoulder and pulled her against him. She was shaking; you could feel her heartbeat right on the surface of her skin.

"Can we go over to the side?" he asked her. "Just to talk?"

"Are the police waiting there?"

"Nobody knows we're here," he murmured. "Nobody."

"Nobody but you?"

"Nobody but me."

"Okay," she said.

"Real slow," he said. "One step at a time." He sidestepped along the dam, guiding her slowly, step by step. Caps of white foam flew up the curtain of churning water.

"You're the only one I ever wanted to tell, Drew. Only you."

"Well you can tell me now. I can be the first person you'll tell. That's a good thing to do." He nested his lips against the side of her face and kissed her warm soft skin. "No matter what, I'll still love you. I promise you that."

She winced as if he'd just hit her. "How could you? No one, not even Troy. No one ever loved me."

"I do," Drew said. He held her around the waist as they took the final steps off the dam. *I did. I did love this girl.*

She fell to her knees, sobbing, and he dropped down with her. "First," he whispered. "Were you there, honey? Were you there when they killed Allison?"

At first she was perfectly still, but then her back softened and she began to nod heavily. "Yes," she whispered. "Yes I was. I was there."

He leaned into her, the line of his body against hers. She'd have to feel him beside her, feel him breathing with her. "Here I am," he murmured. "I'm right here. Did you bring the rope? Was it your rope that you used to tie her up?"

"Yes," she whispered. "I tied her up."

"Here I am," he said gently. He held his palm on her hand. A siren sounded in the distance. "Did you cut her?" he asked. "Bahar, I have to know." He gripped her fingers tight. "Here I am. And I'm not going anywhere." The words came easy, tumbling softly from his lips. He wasn't going anywhere, but it was his choice. And he'd be walking her down this grassy hill no matter how she answered. He'd walk her around the mill. He'd walk her across Redder's Road, over to her house. Eventually, if he had to, he'd walk her right into her jail cell, pull the door shut, and lock it. They both knew that.

Bahar's voice trembled up out of her chest. "Yes, I cut her," she said. "I used Jake's knife."

Drew was silent. He could feel the hole in the air, the place where she expected him to console her. He was aware of every point where his skin touched hers. He opened his mouth. The words failed him.

And now she was slipping away, even as he held her, held her tighter. He couldn't feel her in his arms.

Just then, a gust of wind picked up a net of cold stream-water and lifted it over the dam summit. It fell like an icy rain across his back, but this once he didn't shiver.